D1478777

Snowbound Heart

Maxine Patrick

Thorndike Press • Thorndike, Maine

Library of Congress Cataloging in Publication Data:

Maxwell, Patricia

Patrick, Maxine, 1942-
  Snowbound heart.

  Large print.
  1. Large type books. I. Title.
[PS3563.A923S6 1982]   813'.54   82-16753
ISBN 0-89621-392-7

Large Print edition available through arrangement with The New American Library.

Cover design by Ralph Lizotte.

For Edith, who has a
compassionate heart

1

The snow swirled in the thin mountain air, sweeping soundlessly toward the windshield of the car. It had become much thicker in the past half-hour. With a frown between her wide-spaced gray eyes, Clare Thornton glanced at the wind-driven flakes. She could not claim to know a great deal about snow, since there was little of it to contend with during the winter in the Louisiana lowlands, but the conditions building up around her were beginning to take on an appearance suspiciously like what she had always thought a blizzard must look like. Earlier in the day, the sun had been bright; there had been spectacular views of majestic peaks topped with snow and bottomless valleys aromatic with the smells of pine, spruce, and fir. Now the heavy white clouds had closed in around her. She could barely make out the dark green branches of the trees along the winding road she was following, and despite the fact that she was driving with her headlights on, she was growing increasingly uncertain of where the edge was on this narrow, unpaved track. There was no such thing as a shoulder along it; only a curbing of scraped earth, covered now with snow, marked the verge as a warning to travelers that their wheels were about to spin in open air. When she had first turned onto it a half-hour before, she had thought the steep precipices falling down to frozen streams breathtaking in their magnificence. Now, when she could no longer see them for the thick press of snow, the mere idea made her blood freeze in her veins.

Clare sat forward on her seat to scrub at the windshield. It did no good. The fogging snow obscuring her vision was on the outside; it could not be swept away entirely, even by the clacking windshield wipers. The road was climbing again. She could feel her small car strain to take the grade. How much longer she could keep going without slipping back, she did not know. It would have been nice if the snow chains that resided in the trunk of her vehicle had been on its wheels. Unfortunately, they were not. It only went to show what a greenhorn she was. Beverly had told her to

8

bring them and have them put on at the first sign of bad weather. The only thing was, the weather had been beautiful up until a couple of hours ago, and by that time Clare had been on this labyrinth of back roads. She had thought the darkening of the sky was the onset of dusk, until it was too late.

No doubt Beverly, outspoken and uncompromisingly honest, would have a few words to say about her lack of forethought. Clare would have a choice word or two to say herself, however, on the subject of her friend's ability to draw a map. The squiggling lines hastily scrawled on the back of Beverly's last letter, which had seemed so simple when she left Louisiana two days before, had proven woefully inadequate.

Why on earth had she ever let herself be talked into coming at this time of year? Clare asked herself, not for the first time. The answer was simple, really. Beverly could make anything sound like exciting fun. From the moment the other girl had married her ski instructor after a trip to Aspen and Snowmass the year before, Clare had heard nothing except how marvelous the mountain life was, and how determined Beverly was for Clare to come and experience it firsthand. It didn't matter that Clare had never buckled on a pair of skis; Beverly's husband would teach her all she needed to know. Clare could stay with the two of them in their quaintly rustic log cabin away from the tourist-crowded resort towns. They would enjoy the snow, roaring fires, spiced wine, healthy outdoor exercise, and a large amount of Clare's favorite pastime, people-watching. It was also possible that they would find Clare a man, a nice outdoor type like Beverly's John, who would marry her and keep her there in Colorado, close to Beverly.

By the time her friend had finally made the invitation definite, Clare had run out of excuses. More than that, she had been ready to get away for a few days. She needed to think. It really didn't matter whether she learned to ski or not, nor did it make any difference that Beverly's quaint cabin might turn out to be a bit more primitive than Beverly had made it out to be. She would enjoy seeing Bev and listening to her rattle on in her headlong fashion. She would like meeting John and getting to know the man Bev had married. And it was just possible that in that famous mountain winter quiet she could find time to decide what she was going to do with her future.

The problem was, the job she had now, as a secretary in a real-estate office, had too much promise. In another year or so she would know enough about the business to take the state examination and get her own license. The policy toward women in the office was progressive; she knew she would be treated fairly. In five years' time she could be making as much on sales commissions as any man in the office. On the other hand, there was her writing. For the past seven months she had been doing articles, warm human-interest stories, for the largest newspaper in town. She had not made a lot of money, but she had enjoyed doing them, and they had given her the right to call herself a freelance writer. A few days before Clare had received Beverly's letter, she had been offered a position in the Life-style section of the newspaper. It seemed like a great opportunity to make a living doing something that gave her pleasure, and earn more money than she could expect in her present job for some time. The only drawback was, she was not certain she would be allowed to write the kind of in-depth pieces she preferred. She was afraid "Life-style" was no more than a euphemism for the women's section. There was nothing wrong with that, of course, if she were willing to settle for paraphrasing endless descriptions of society weddings, cotillions, and charity bazaars. She was not sure she was willing. She

11

knew well enough that she had a certain facility with words, but did her ability to write amount to no more than that? She did not know. Beverly, despite her enthusiasms and impulsive ways, was well above average intelligence. Moreover, she was not chary with the truth. Her opinion on anything was worth having. For that reason, just before she had left home Clare had thrust the tear sheets of the articles that had appeared in the paper into the side pocket of the canvas tote that served her as a handbag. She would let Bev read them. Who could tell? It was always possible she was every bit as good a writer as she thought, in which case a whole new career might present itself!

Abruptly the grin flitting across Clare's finely molded mouth faded. She braked to a halt. The road she was following had come to a dead end before the dark bulk of a house. Set back from the highway right-of-way, it rose among the evergreens, a steep-roofed chalet with a balcony wrapped around it at treetop level and a wide lower deck. It was visible for no more than an instant; then it was gone, hidden in the blowing snow.

Clare leaned back, running her fingers through the long strands of her sun-streaked blond hair with a defeated sigh. She had been so sure this was the right road, that it must eventually bring her to Beverly's and John's cabin. She had been wrong. The mountain home before her could not by any stretch of the imagination be their simple cabin with the bark still on the logs. The truth was, she was lost. She would have to make her way back to Aspen, call Bev, and ask her to lead her to the cabin. It was what she should have done in the first place.

It was getting late. Already the light was fading. If she didn't turn up before dark, Bev would be worried. She was expecting Clare for dinner. The trip should not take more than two days, Bev had assured her blithely, even if Clare stopped to read every historical marker along the way, as she was almost certain to do. Bev had not taken a blizzard into account. She had not even mentioned the possibility of bad weather when Clare had called her the night before she left.

Could she make her way back the way she had come? She would have to try. So far as she had been able to see, the house before was deserted, empty. No doubt it was a summer place, closed now for the winter. There had been no sign of a light in the windows, no cars or other vehicles before it. Beverly had spoken often of such houses, open during the summer for vacationing families, then shut up at the first snowfall and all telephone and electric service disconnected. Sometimes they were opened for a week or so of skiing around the Christmas holidays, but it did not appear that was the case here. She could expect no help from that quarter.

The snow was beginning to pile in drifts in the clearing of the drive before the house. Backing and turning was no easy matter. As she felt her tires slip in the compacted ruts of her own makings, Clare clenched her teeth. She was in trouble and she knew it. The only thing she did not know was the best thing to do about it. She could stop the car and sit where she was until help came, but how long would that be on this little-traveled back road? The gas to keep the motor running to warm the car would last only so long. She had a heavy coat and a suitcase full of warm clothes with her, but she was far from certain they would be sufficient against the bitter cold she felt hovering outside the warm interior of the car. Moreover, she had no food, not even a bar of candy. No doubt it was foolish of her to be so unprepared, and yet when she had left her motel room in Texas early that morning, the sun had been shining and the temperature in the high forties. It was unbelievable the change a few hundred miles could make.

A few minutes could make a change also. In the time it had taken her to turn and start back down the road, her car's tracks had been obliterated, covered by a soft blanket of white. The deepening snow had leveled the roadbed, hiding the banked ridge that marked the edge, making it blend with the flying fog of snow that whipped around the car, enveloping it.

Clare's nerves jerked as she strained to see. In the smothering quiet, the whispering sigh of the wind seemed louder than the hum of her car's motor as it crept along. Then she felt the slant of a downhill grade. The road would be curving to the left, she knew; still, ahead of her was nothing but a white-walled tunnel without end. Instinctively she put her foot on the brake. For an instant the car checked; then it began to slide, and Clare felt the banked ridge at the far side as her front tire struck it. She wrenched the steering wheel to the left. The back of the car slewed around, and the right-rear tire dropped over the edge. Clare was flung hard to the side against her shoulder harness. The steering wheel was jerked from her grasp, and then it was as though she were being dragged backward down the side of the mountain. The car tilted, beginning to roll. Suddenly it came to a thudding, teeth-jarring stop. Wood cracked with an icy explosion like a gunshot, and hard on the sound came a cold tinkle of broken glass. The breath left Clare's lungs as she was thrown back against the seat.

By the time she could breathe again, everything was quiet once more. Her car was sitting half-buried in snow with the hood pointed into the air and the side doors bent around a giant ponderosa pine. The sharp smell of resin filled the air where branches had been broken away, and through the smashed window came clean, cold air laden with powdery eddies of snow.

Automatically Clare reached and turned the key, cutting off the motor. With trembling fingers she unfastened her seat belt, slipped from the harness, and reached for her canvas tote and camel's hair coat on the seat beside her. The cream sweater, green corduroy skirt, and calf-length boots she wore had not been meant for weather conditions like these. It could not be helped. She could not stay in the car. At any moment the gas tank might explode. Freezing was preferable to a fiery death.

For an instant she thought the door on the driver's side of the car would not open. Holding the handle with both hands, she heaved herself against it once, twice. It flew wide, and she tumbled out, sinking in snow above her ankles. Pushing away from the car, she shoved the door shut and retreated a few feet, slipping on

16

the steep grade. Gaining her balance, she struggled into her coat and tied the belt around her waist. A shudder ran over her as she swayed in the chill wind. There did not appear to be any immediate danger of fire; still, she did not dare approach the car to retrieve her suitcase. Nor could she stay where she was. Slinging the strap of her bag over her shoulder, she turned away and began to scramble back up the mountainside to the road above her. She had to hurry. The tracks left by the tires of her car would be filling once more, and she needed them to guide her back to the house at the end of the road.

By the time the dark shape of the chalet appeared before her, the ends of her fingers and her toes were numb, and her face was whipped red and raw by the wind. The hem of her long coat was matted with snow, and flakes of it were caught like tiny frozen stars in the long blond strands of her hair. She stumbled a little in the deepening snow as she moved toward the front entrance. She could not prevent herself from running the last few yards that carried her up the ice-and-snow-covered steps and across the long lower deck. Taking a deep breath, she lifted her hand and knocked on the door. While she waited, she glanced around her. The afternoon light had taken on a blue-gray cast, especially here around the house, in a shadow of the evergreens. Soon the swift mountain night would fall.

There was no answer to her repeated knocking. She hesitated a moment; then, with the lovely curves of her mouth set in grim lines, she moved around the deck to the side of the house. Here were sliding glass doors backed by the white lining of draperies. Her knuckles made a sharper, more insistent sound on the cold glass; still no one came. The door was locked, securely locked. Clare moved on. Another set of glass doors, these also locked. How much would it take to break the long double panes? she wondered. She might have to find out.

At the rear of the house, she stopped. More glass doors overlooked the deck, while above them rose a towering wall of glass to the peaked roof of the chalet. Before it, the deck was pointed like the prow of a ship, designed obviously to take advantage of a view, though so far as Clare could see, it jutted out over nothing except a yawning chasm filled with white snow clouds.

Continuing along to the far side of the house, she came to a blank wall that faced onto the evergreen woods. Set into it were a number of high windows and a single steel-clad door. She was about to turn away when on impulse she stepped to this formidable entranceway and tried the handle. It turned under her hand.

Her success was so unexpected that she stood for a full minute staring at it before she even tried to push the heavy panel open. Noiselessly, easily, it swung wide. Clare stepped inside.

She stood in a laundry room. A cocoa mat lay before the door, protecting a floor of polished tiles. Gleaming appliances lined one wall, while on the other was a sink of stainless steel and chrome. Staring about her, Clare stamped the snow from her boots and brushed it from the folds of her coat. Finally she closed the door behind her.

Compared to the windblown chill outside, it felt warm in the house. The sudden quiet away from the sighing and thrashing of the fir and spruce overhead had an unnatural feeling about it. Clare, as she started toward the open door at the other end of the laundry, found herself moving with almost stealthy footsteps.

The laundry opened into a compact modern kitchen with shining wood cabinets. To one side was a table with a Tiffany-style lamp of cut glass in shades of dark green, rust-red, and amber hanging above it. Beyond stretched an enormous living area. The floor was covered with deep pile carpet that rolled in rust-brown waves to a massive moss-rock fireplace, the chimney of which soared up into the cathedral ceiling. With the draperies closed, it was dim inside the room, lit only by the fading light coming through the expanse of glass that reached to the apex of the roof. She could just barely make out a spiral staircase that wound upward to a balcony overlooking the living area, and a row of doors that must be bedrooms.

"Hello!" Clare called. "Is anyone here?" Her voice echoed in the lofty space, but no one answered.

"Hello?" she called again, standing still with her hands in her pockets as she gazed around her. Nothing stirred in the deepening shadows of the great open room. With slow steps, almost as if she were mesmerized, she put her foot out onto the carpet and walked toward the yawning black opening of the fireplace. Coming to a stop before it, she caught her bottom lip between her teeth. She did not like the idea of trespassing, nor using things that did not belong to her, but she had to have shelter. She needed warmth and food or she would die. It was as simple as that. The apologies would have to come later.

Beside the fireplace there was a woodbox

with kindling, and a fair supply of logs stacked inside. Matches hung in a wrought-iron holder beside the massive mantelpiece. Laying a fire was no problem. Until she had moved into an apartment of her own, Clare had lived with her mother and father in a rambling Victorian house that had boasted a fireplace in every room. The wood in the box was pine, which seemed strange to Clare, who was used to oak. Pine, considered too fast-burning for firewood, was reserved for commercial use in Louisiana, for making paper and plywood. The dry, light-weight lengths, would doubtless be easier to get to burn, no small consideration at this moment.

She was right. Within minutes, yellow-orange flames licked at the pine. Kneeling on the hearth, Clare stretched her hands to the blaze. As the heat grew, she felt the tight knot of apprehension in her chest begin to dissolve. Not only was there wood in the box, she had noticed a large stack of split logs under the decking at the front of the house. She could stay here for some time if she had to. She disliked the idea of worrying Beverly, but she could do nothing about it. For tonight she was all right; tomorrow would have to take care of itself.

"Tonight" was the right word. In the short

time it had taken for her to lay the fire and get it burning brightly, darkness had descended. Clare got stiffly to her feet. Outside, she could still hear the whine and rush of the snowstorm. On such a night, the best place for her to sleep would be in front of the fire. Since she had dared so much already, she might as well go a little further and see if there were blankets to be found in the upstairs bedrooms. She should have thought of that before night fell, of course. Now she would have to manage a light of some kind.

There was always the possibility that there was a flashlight or candles in the house, if she could only find them. The best place to start looking was in the kitchen, and if she should happen to come across something to still the pangs of hunger beginning to make themselves felt in her midsection, she did not think that she would have the willpower to resist.

The first cabinet door she opened held a supply of paper plates and cups, items not unreasonable for a summer place. The second held canned goods, also expected, though the supply seemed overgenerous to have been left from summer. The third cabinet held dishes, simple brown ironstone, but in the fourth was something that brought Clare to a halt. It was bread wrapped in cellophane, bread as soft and fresh as if it had just come from the bakery. Clare pressed it gingerly, then drew back her hand. Taking a deep breath, she closed the cabinet door, then turned toward the gleam of the refrigerator. Grasping the handle, she pulled it open.

The appliance light came on instantly, throwing its cool white glare into the room, illuminating shelves holding milk, cheese, juice, bacon, meat, fruit – anything a hungry person might crave.

The implication of the food and the glowing light inside the refrigerator held her stunned. In that instant a sound came from the direction of the laundry room. She heard the opening of the door, the scrape of the cocoa mat, and then, as she turned in that direction, a man, tall and broad in heavy clothing crusted with snow, swung into view.

At the sight of her he stopped, a scowl drawing thick blond brows together. "What the devil . . . ?" he exclaimed.

Clare's grip on the handle of the refrigerator tightened until her knuckles gleamed white. "I . . . I'm sorry," she said hurriedly. "I thought the house was empty."

"Did you now?" the man asked. His voice was soft, but the bite of sarcasm in it was so stinging that she flinched.

"Yes. I didn't mean to trespass, but the door was open, and I had nowhere else to go."

"You could not have left the same way you arrived? I am assuming, naturally, that you didn't walk all the way up here."

Clare shook her head, her gray eyes anxious in her effort to make him understand. "No, I couldn't. I got caught in the snowstorm. My car skidded, and I went off the road."

"Careless of you," he drawled, and began to tug off his fur-lined gloves.

"Careless?" Clare repeated slowly, the anger stirring inside her at his complete lack of concern for her confusion. "It was unlucky, yes, even unwise, but I don't think it was careless."

"And I can't quite think it was entirely unlucky, since it landed you on my doorstep."

"You sound as if you think I did it on purpose! Believe me, stranding myself in such an isolated place with a strange man in the midst of a blizzard is the last thing I would think of doing." Before the words had left her lips, he laughed in real amusement, a sound that rang in her ears with an odd and disturbing familiarity.

"A good try, but not good enough." As he spoke, he reached up to pull off the heavy cap that covered his hair and toss it with his gloves to the kitchen counter. "If you really have wrecked your car to get in here, I won't throw you out on your ear in this weather, as much as I might like to. You may as well be honest, and admit this is exactly the way you planned it."

"Honest . . .?" Clare began, a frown drawing her brows together as she stared at him in wrath and perplexity. "I don't know what you . . ."

As he turned full-face to her, she stopped. The firelight from across the room caught in his hair, sliding across its fine sculptured waves with the soft sheen of pure gold. It touched the gold tips of his lashes, the only feminine thing in the strong mold of his features, and glinted with pinpoints of fire in the vivid blue of his eyes. The beguiling smile known to millions of women curved his mouth. That it was touched with mockery did not make it any less effective.

"Logan Longcross," Clare whispered on an indrawn breath. Understanding flooded over her in a wave. Logan Longcross, superstar, a movie idol, who could demand and get better than three million dollars for every picture he made, a major box-office attraction famous for his slow smile, for the sensitivity he brought to the roles he played, and for his intense dislike of the notoriety thrust upon him, with its corresponding lack of privacy.

"Yeah," he agreed, the single word clipped and sarcastic.

"I see," she said. "You think I am here because of a schoolgirlish case of star worship? Let me assure you I am no groupie desperate to be near you!"

He frowned judiciously. "Not bad," he said, "but the outrage is just a bit overdone, and you forgot to accuse me of conceit."

"I was just coming to that," Clare retorted, her gray eyes stormy.

"I'm sure you were, and it might be a good idea to throw in another insult or two for good measure. You must not, under any circumstances, show that I have any attraction for you. That would be as good as admitting your guilt." As he spoke, he stepped closer. Placing his hand on the refrigerator door, he drew it gently from her grasp and let it fall shut.

"There is no danger of that," Clare said with a lift of her chin. She got no further. Before she could move, before she could even guess his intention, he reached out with sure strength and pulled her against him. His blue gaze, narrowed in speculation, held her for an instant, and then his mouth came down on hers. Shock held her motionless under the burning pressure, and then, as she recognized the leashed contempt and deliberate testing of her weakness that drove him, she brought up her hands and pushed him from her.

He released her and stepped back. Surveying her flushed face and tight-pressed lips, he lifted an eyebrow. "Score another point in your favor. I could almost believe you neither expected nor wanted that."

Clare drew a deep, trembling breath. "Of all the arrogant, self-satisfied men I have ever met, you are the worst!"

"Self-satisfied? I think there is a distinction between the attraction I might have as a man and the fascination women like you find in big-name entertainers. Whatever it is that has brought you here has more to do with the publicity department of the movie studio than it does with me. I fail to see why you think that would give me any satisfaction."

Logan Longcross had no monopoly on sarcasm. Clare allowed herself to smile. "Next you will be saying your star image is a burden that you never wanted."

"That's right," he said, his voice hard. "I wanted to be good at my job, to move people to laughter or to tears, to make them think. I wanted respect, not this overblown glorification." Abruptly a tight, controlled look descended over his features. "Never mind. If you want to pretend to be a young woman thrown into my company for a night through misfortune, then that is the way we will play it.

It won't make any difference in the long run."

"I promise you this is no game for me," Clare said.

"No, of course not," he agreed, his voice much too grave. "You may as well take off your coat too and be comfortable. Here, let me turn the light on for you. You will be surprised how much easier it is to make yourself at home if you can see what you are doing."

In the process of shrugging out of his insulated jacket, he swung toward the light switch on the far wall. His sleeve caught the strap of Clare's canvas tote she had left sitting on the end of the counter, and sent it toppling toward the floor. Even as it fell, he swung with lightning reflexes to catch it. Only the sheaf of tear sheets Clare had pushed into the side pocket for Beverly spilled out, fluttering to the floor.

With a muffled oath Logan flipped on the light, then bent to retrieve her papers. He straightened with them in his hand, turning as though he meant to pass them over as she stepped forward. Her fingers had closed on them when his grip suddenly tightened.

"Who," he asked softly, his gaze on her by-line, "is Clare Thornton?"

"I am," Clare answered, made wary by something in his manner, despite the quiet, even timbre of his voice.

"At least there is something you will admit."

As Clare met his eyes, she caught her breath at the temper she saw blazing in their bright blue depths. "I am a free-lance writer, if that is what you mean."

"A free-lance with ambition, or so it seems. I believe I owe you an apology. You were telling the truth when you said you were no fan of mine. Your purpose in coming here was not nearly so straightforward. Tell me, what did you mean to call the article you were going to write? 'I Spent the Night with Logan Longcross'? 'I Discovered Logan's Mountain Retreat'?"

The kind of sensation journalism he was talking about, the kind found usually in movie magazines of the less respectable sort and in supermarket tabloids, was so unlike the articles Clare usually wrote that she could only stare at him in speechless indignation.

"What is the matter? Can't you come up with an explanation that will prove your innocence and still let you get on with your story?"

"If you will look over these tear sheets, you will see that my writing is nothing like what you have in mind. You will also see that the people I interview are not famous; they are just ordinary people who have managed to contribute something of themselves to make the lives of others easier or richer. Even if I had decided to try to speak to someone like you, I would have gone through regular channels, made inquiries, put a request in writing."

"And you would have been turned down, as you well know. Except for publicity material for new releases, I don't give interviews."

"This may come as a surprise, but I didn't know, not that it matters. The point is, I would never do anything so stupid as to try to see you in such a sneaking, underhanded way. Even if I did, I think I would have better sense than to bring a bundle of tear sheets advertising my profession with me!"

"I don't know about that. The members of your profession, as you call it, have not been noted for their ethics or their intelligence."

The bitterness in his words touched off a slow-moving chain of memory. Hadn't there been mention of Logan Longcross in the gossip columns lately? If she remembered correctly, he had been charged with assaulting a photographer who was trying to take unauthorized pictures of the actor and the woman who had been with him at the time. There had been much speculation as to his relationship with the woman, because of his attempt to protect her. She had been identified as the wife of a noted producer. Clare thought that the charges had been dropped later, but the newspapers, and especially the weekly tabloids, had enjoyed a field day. Logan Longcross was so seldom seen in public, so seldom attracted attention to himself, that they had made the most of it.

Her face stiff, Clare took her tear sheets from him and reached out her hand for her tote bag. "I understand how you must feel," she said more quietly. "All I can do is repeat what I said before. I had an accident while trying to find the cabin of a friend. I came back here, found the place deserted and the back door unlocked. I assumed the house was empty for the winter, and took shelter. I had only just discovered my mistake when I heard you come in. Until then, I had not realized the electric power was on in the house."

"Despite the fact that the central heat, though on a low setting while I was out, still has kept this place quite a few degrees warmer than it is outside."

"I noticed some difference, but I thought it was because I was so cold and shaken. What I am trying to get at is this: if you have electric power, you must have a telephone also. If you will let me use it, I will call my friend. It is possible she and her husband will have some kind of vehicle equipped for this kind of weather. They may be able to come and take me off your hands."

"A fine plan," he said, throwing the jacket he had removed onto the countertop, "except for one thing. I didn't bother to have the phone connected for the few days I plan on being here."

The wind whipped around the outside of the house. The snow driven against the exposed glass of the living area made a soft, whispering sound. To Clare it seemed as if the strength of the blizzard was increasing. She glanced at the man beside her, her gray eyes measuring and her soft lips compressed. After a moment she said, "I suppose you flew in from California to Aspen, but you must have driven up here."

"If you are suggesting that I could take you back to Aspen, or anywhere else, you can forget it. I drove up here, all right, in a rental car. It has snow tires, and chains are available, but as much as I might like to see you on your way, I don't intend to risk wrecking it on a night like this for the pleasure."

"In that case, it looks like you are stuck with me," she said, her tone flat.

"So it does, and now that we have made our positions clear, maybe we had better start making the best of them. I would say, from the way you were poking around in the kitchen, that you must be hungry. I know I am starving."

It was, in its own way, an offer of a truce, though an armed one. To refuse was tempting, but Clare, her knees weak from hunger and the exhaustion of shock, could not bring herself to do it. "How can I turn down such gracious hospitality?" she replied, and smiled sweetly as he flung her a quick frown.

It was at that moment that the lights in the kitchen flickered once and went out, leaving them standing in darkness.

2

Their evening meal consisted of sandwich meat and cheese wrapped in bread, beer for Logan, and a soft drink for Clare. They spread the feast on the carpet before the fireplace, not only for the light, but also for the warmth. The power failure had put an end to the central heat. Before half an hour had passed, the intense cold had begun to penetrate into the house, making the blazing fire seem precious. They ate in silence. Once or twice Clare glanced at her reluctant host. His face, bronzed by the firelight, was so grim that she did not think it wise to call attention to herself, even if she could have come up with a neutral subject for conversation.

Cleaning up, when they had finished their meal, was a simple matter of crumpling their paper napkins and cups and tossing them into the fire. Clare sat watching the plastic-foam cups melt and the napkins turn to gray ash. At last, unable to bear the uncomfortable stillness, she got to her feet and moved to the sliding doors. She lifted the curtain and peered out. There was nothing but mesh screen. The snow still fell, sweeping with tiny scraping noises against the wood siding of the house, muffling, deadening the ceaseless soughing of the evergreens overhead.

Clare shivered a little, wrapping her coat closer around her. The situation she had landed herself in was beyond belief. She felt like an idiot, and yet she did not know what else she could have done. She supposed if she had been experienced in mountain driving or with snow, she might have taken some action such as having her snow chains mounted before the emergency arose. She did not like to admit it, but it was true. So much for her claim, made often in the past couple of years since her parents had died, of being able to take care of herself. She had never felt less self-sufficient than at this moment. It did not take much to get into trouble, after all: only a little ignorance, a bit too much trust in luck. She would like to keep this episode to herself, but she doubted it would be possible. Beverly was too quick to be taken in by any trumped-up tale. On the other hand, Clare told herself wryly, it might be worth the exclaiming and teasing she would have to endure just to be able to tell someone exactly what had taken place, and what she thought of the arrogant and surly actor.

Behind her, Logan got to his feet and went to rummage in the kitchen cabinets. With a jar of roasted peanuts in his hand he crossed the room and stood with his back to the flames. Clare heard the sound of the jar opening. A moment later, he spoke.

"What are you doing over there? Come back to the fire before you are chilled to the bone."

Clare swung around to find Logan watching her. "I can't think what concern it is of yours."

"I would just as soon not have to cope with pneumonia."

"I expect not, especially since it might delay my leaving."

He made no reply, but neither did he remove his compelling blue gaze. Clare hesitated an instant; then, feeling the cold at her back, she moved toward him, taking her seat once more before the hearth. He offered the peanuts with a silent gesture, and she took a few in the palm of her hand.

The minutes passed. Logan bent to put another length of wood on the fire; then he stepped to the deep pillow couch of brown velour that sat in the far corner of the room. Scooping up several of the large, overstuffed cushions, he brought them and threw them down beside Clare. "I strongly suspect, since the power is still out, that a tree or dead limb must have gone down on the lines. That happens more often out here than any kind of municipal outage. In this weather, it will probably be a while before anyone can get to it. We might as well make ourselves comfortable."

"I guess so," Clare said, slanting him an upward glance. "Before you sit down, though, don't you think you should put your jacket back on? I'm no more anxious to take on the duties of a nurse than you are, contrary to what you might think."

He shook his head. Reaching for the peanut jar, he let himself down on the cushion beside her. "I'm a little better dressed for the cold than you are, since I planned on being out in it. I still have another layer under these." He indicated the flannel shirt and jeans he wore. "But if that last remark of yours means what I think it does, let me tell you that I am well aware that for every woman who might like to soothe my fevered brow, there are a hundred who wonder why they don't make leading men like they used to, dark and dashing."

Clare's mouth curved in an unbidden smile. That he had a sense of humor should not have been surprising; it flashed out often enough on the screen. To have it surface through his very real exasperation was unexpected. She tilted her head to one side. "So you do admit there are women who might not consider it the thrill of a lifetime to be stranded with you?"

"Oh, yes, I admit it," he said scathingly. "But I can always be certain that before my ego shrinks too badly some sweet young thing will stow away in my dressing trailer and pop into the bathroom just as I am beginning to shave, or else fling herself at me and tear the lapel off of a six-hundred-dollar suit."

"I suppose it is to escape such annoyances that you come here?"

"Among other things," he answered with a sardonic glance that plainly indicated he thought he was being pumped for information. "Ordinarily, it is safe enough. Which brings another question to mind. I was under the impression that no one knew about this house except my agent. Since I am fairly sure he would not give out the information without good reason, just how the devil did you find it?"

Clare watched as he took up the poker and gave a savage jab to a smoldering log. "You won't accept that it was sheer coincidence?"

"No," he said shortly.

"Well, let me see how I might have gone about it, then. Perhaps I saw you in town and followed you back to your lair?"

"You might have, except I haven't been anywhere near Aspen since I landed at the airport a week ago. It certainly took you a long time to catch up."

"Hummm. Perhaps I was looking over the land records to see which celebrities had property in the area and just happened to come across your name?"

"You might, except I had the foresight to put the title in my parents' name."

"Your parents? Do they live in the area?"

"No. They come up for a few weeks in the summer to give the place a good airing. That is all the information you will get on them. You may as well drop that lead, and answer my question."

"You mean how I ran you to earth?" Clare asked in mock innocence, then went on hurriedly as he turned slowly to stare at her. "Yes, I think I must have cornered your agent at one of those famous Hollywood parties and charmed him so that he told me all I wanted to know."

"That is just possible," he said. "A short

man, round and balding, was he?"

"Yes, I believe he was."

"Then you talked to the wrong man. My agent is tall and in possession of a full head of gray hair."

Clare clicked her tongue. "Undoubtedly the wrong man. I wonder how I came to make such a mistake?"

"So do I," Logan said, his tone dry.

Sternly controlling the urge to grin, Clare frowned at the burning logs in the fireplace. "I think that exhausts every possible way I might have found you. Don't you think it must have been an accident, then?"

Greatly daring, she turned her head to look at him. He was watching her, his gaze on the shining curtain of her hair glinting silver-gold in the firelight. His deep blue gaze searched the pure oval of her face. As he met her gray eyes, her steady gaze did not waver, not even as his own narrowed in sudden consideration.

"No," he answered finally, a pensive note in his low voice, "though as strange as it may seem, I almost wish I could."

It was Clare who looked away first. An uncomfortable silence stretched between them. The need to break it, to change the subject that had suddenly grown too personal, forced her into speech. "Where were you this evening

40

when I stumbled in here? After what you said about your car just now, I don't suppose you were far away."

"No, I was out walking. I needed to exercise, and it helps me to think. The house here overlooks a gorge with a stream at the bottom. There's a trail that winds down to it, if you don't mind the climb back up again. It was snowing when I started out just after noon, but I hadn't been listening to the weather reports, hadn't so much as turned on a radio since I have been here. I never expected it to turn nasty as fast as it did, or I would not have gone so far."

"I didn't expect it, either. I heard the forecast on the car radio earlier in the afternoon. Snow was predicted, but I didn't know it was going to be like this, almost like a blizzard."

"My dear girl, this is not almost a blizzard, this *is* one!"

"Is it? I wasn't sure. Where I come from we don't have such things. Hurricanes, yes, and tornadoes, but no blizzards."

"Where do you come from?"

Clare told him, adding, in defiance of the skepticism in his expression, a fuller explanation of her reasons for being in the ski country. Logan did not comment. On reflection, Clare decided that was a good sign. He might not

41

believe what she said; still, she thought he did not entirely disbelieve it either, or he would definitely have had something to say.

The fire crackled in the quiet. Clare stared into the flames, watching the pulsating glow of the red coals. Despite the cold she could feel at her back, gathering beyond the radius of the fireplace, she felt warm. The blessed heat seemed to soak into her skin, reminding her of the long miles she had traveled that day. She was more tired than she had realized until that moment. There was a sore place on her shoulder where the restraining harness of her seat belt had caught her, and though she did not remember bumping her head when the car went down the embankment, there was a spot with the tenderness of a bruise on her temple just at the hairline. Without warning, a yawn gripped her, and she smothered it with a slight shake of her head.

Logan tossed the last of his peanuts into his mouth and brushed the salt from his hands onto the fire. "It's time we started thinking about sleeping arrangements," he said, his words casual and yet tinged with irony. "I think our best bet is to make up beds here in front of the fire."

"You mean right here, both of us?"

"That's right, unless you would rather freeze

to death, and I mean just that. To my certain knowledge, there are only a half-dozen blankets in the house. That may sound adequate, but of the six, three are light-weight, suitable for the cool nights we get up here in the summer. The other three are electric."

"I see what you mean," Clare said slowly. As long as the power was off, the electric controls were useless. If they divided the blankets between them, someone was going to wind up with two light pieces of cover. That would not do, not in temperatures well below freezing. What was needed was not only blankets, but several down comforters, or else a nice heated room. Lacking either, they could share the blankets — or make beds before the fire. She grimaced. "The cushions should make a fairly soft bed. Now, if we only had a nice electric alarm clock, we could set it to wake us every two or three hours so we can keep the fire burning."

"I doubt either one of us will sleep so soundly we can't keep up with that chore. We will need more wood, though. Here, you take this." He handed her the flashlight from his coat pocket. "If you will see to the sleeping arrangements, I will fill the woodbox."

It was not exactly a fair division of the labor, Clare thought as she watched him button his jacket and plunge out into the cold, blowing snow; still, she was grateful. Whether it was tact or common sense that had made him leave the placing of the bedding to her, she was glad she did not have to do it under his sardonic gaze.

It was not difficult to find the blankets he had mentioned, though she had to strip two of them from the bed in the room where he had been sleeping. It took two trips up the spiral staircase to bring down the cover and linens they would need. On impulse, she ran back up again to fetch a pair of pillows. They did not need them, precisely, but she saw no reason why they should not be as comfortable as possible.

She was just rounding the last turn of the stairs when Logan appeared, his arms piled high with wood, from the direction of the kitchen. She stopped, hugging the pillows with one arm while she held the flashlight in her other hand. Logan stopped also, waiting for her to cross in front of him. For no reason that she could think of, Clare felt the heat of a flush rising to her face as their eyes caught and held. With a fervent hope that he had not noticed her confusion in the dimness, she gave a faint smile and continued toward the fireplace. It was a relief when she heard his footsteps on the kitchen tiles and the door closing behind him once more.

What was the matter with her? Clare took herself to task as she hurriedly pushed cushions into place, spread sheets and blankets over them, and tossed pillows on the ends of the makeshift beds so that their feet would be nearer the flames. She was willing to admit that Logan Longcross was an attractive man, possibly even more than attractive. The situation was not one you ran into every day. Still, there was no reason to be upset. By tomorrow, the weather would be clear again. She could be on her way, and all this would be forgotten. It was the aftereffects of her accident and the strangeness of the snowstorm that had set her nerves on edge. The prospect of spending the night alone with a man, and that man Logan Longcross, did not daunt her, not at all.

For long moments she stood staring down at the makeshift beds; then, stopping swiftly, she pushed them a few inches farther apart.

By the time Logan returned with his last load of firewood, Clare had unzipped her boots and slipped them off, and was kneeling to poke up the fire. She moved to one side as Logan placed an enormous log on the andirons.

Logan glanced at her. "A backlog," he said in answer to her look of inquiry. "With any luck, it should keep going long enough for us to get a little sleep."

Clare nodded her comprehension, watching as he put more wood on top of the larger log, placing it with quick competence. She took a deep breath. "I have no night things with me, but I suppose it is just as well. We will probably be better off sleeping in our clothes, anyway."

Logan made a sound that might have been an assent. Clare thought he flung a glance in her direction, but since she was carefully avoiding looking at him, she could not be certain. Standing the poker in its holder, she turned away, moving to seat herself on the end of one of the beds.

"I'll take that one," Logan said.

"Oh, but —"

"It is closer to the woodbox."

It was also the one with the lightweight blankets on it. "It doesn't matter," Clare said. "I'll take my turn feeding the fire."

"There's no need."

"There is every need. I want to do my share."

Logan swung to face her, still on one knee, with his forearm resting across the other. "I appreciate the offer," he said deliberately, "but I would just as soon you made no sacrifices for me. Let me point out again that I am dressed a good deal warmer than you are. On top of that, I am used to the cold, and you are not."

What he said made sense. Combined with the hint that she was trying to make him feel some obligation with her sacrifice, it was enough to make her transfer without another word to the other bed. Throwing back the blankets, she stretched out, then drew them back up over her shoulder as she deliberately turned on her side, facing away from him. For long moments she lay stiff and straight, watching the dancing fire shadows on the walls, uncomfortably aware of the man behind her. Her mind churned in futile fury; Logan Longcross was so sure of himself, so certain he was right about her. Arrogant, overbearing man. After this, he could call himself lucky if she troubled to see another one of his movies. How many had she seen? Three? Four? She could well remember the first. He had not been well known then; the actress who was his leading lady was supposed to have been the star. Slowly, quietly, with his appearance, the power and sensitivity of his performance, and the perfection he brought to the character he played, he had dominated the movie. Clare, scarcely more than a teenager at the time, had looked for his name in the credits when the film was over. She was not the only one. The parts offered to him after that became bigger and better, until the name of Logan Longcross had become a household word, the symbol of a man many women called flawless, while others loved him for his flaws. Clare had not been immune to the magnetism she felt when she sat watching the movie screen in the darkened theater. Nor was she unaware of it now that she had met him in person. Not that it mattered. The fact that she had been able to think of little else meant nothing. If she had been forced into such close quarters with any other man, no doubt she should have given him a large share of her attention also.

Discovering she was uncomfortable, Clare turned to her back. She lifted her eyelids a fraction, then let them fall again. Logan still sat before the fire, staring into the flames. Bronzed, burnished, self-contained, he had the aloofness of a man who neither needed nor wanted anyone to share his solitude. Perhaps it was not so strange he had never married. There had been the producer's wife, however, the woman who had been accorded his protection from unwanted publicity. What was she to him, Clare wondered, that he had gone to such lengths to prevent any intrusion upon their moments together?

It was not the producer's wife that occupied

Clare's thoughts in the moments before she slept, however. It was the memory of Logan's lips on hers.

Morning was slow in coming. Gray-white snow clouds still pressed close to the house when Clare slid from her bed. In stocking feet she padded about, searching in the kitchen for a frying pan and a pot that did not look as if setting them in the coals of the fireplace would ruin them. The stainless-steel cookware she found would take the punishment, she knew, but she did not think it would ever look the same again. There was no other choice. They had to eat, and it was not as if Logan could not afford to replace anything damaged in such a good cause.

There was a drip coffeepot in one of the cabinets, but since the power failure seemed to have something to do with the water supply, she would have to go outside for snow to melt before she could make coffee. Clare had picked up the pot and started toward the sliding doors when Logan spoke from the darkened living area.

"Here," he said, pulling on his heavy, insulated boots. "I'll do that."

Clare drew a sharp breath, coming to a halt. "I didn't mean to wake you."

"You didn't," he said.

That short answer seemed plain enough. They were to be no more friendly this morning than they had been the night before. Without another word Clare put the pot she held down on the end of the dining table and turned back to the kitchen.

Coffee, bacon, eggs, and toast lightly browned on one side, only slightly burned on the other, was their breakfast. Clare cooked it kneeling before the fire with her face growing red from the heat. They ate it from the top of a coffee table that Logan dragged up before the warmth, using their neatly tucked-up beds for seats.

Holding out his cup for a refill, Logan gave a slight smile. "I suppose since I had to be snowed in with a representative of the press, it is worth something that you can cook."

"You are too kind," Clare murmured, her tone dry as she tilted the pot above his cup.

"Probably so," he agreed. "It wouldn't do to encourage you."

"I don't think there is any danger of that."

Logan made no answer, but the look he sent her was long and searching.

The snow still fell in a thick curtain that was shaken and lifted, then let fall again by the keening wind. The soft whiteness drifted across the decks of the house in deep piles and lay heaped against the glass door. Dressed once more in coat and boots, Clare moved from one to the other of the door and window openings, with their curtains flung open for light, watching in fascination. There was nothing to be seen but the falling flakes and the dark outlines of the evergreens. Everything else was lost in the encroaching snow. Still Clare stared out. She had never seen so much snow, had never known it to fall with such endless persistence, as though it meant never to stop, as if it meant to bury them in soft, feathery cold.

Teeth clenched in determination, she had helped Logan bring in a fresh supply of wood. Together they had cleared away the breakfast things, wiping the grease from the skillet with a handful of paper towels, then burning them with the paper cups and plates. Afterward, she had managed to freshen her appearance, using the cosmetics in her tote bag and water heated in a metal bucket from the laundry. With those few tasks out of the way, there was nothing else to do; she might as well watch the snow.

In the room behind her, Logan was reading; a screenplay, she thought, from the way it was bound and the notes he made now and then in the margin. She had not liked to ask. She would give the man no excuse to accuse her of prying. He had offered her a collection of magazines his mother had left behind the summer before, but Clare could not settle down with them. Fashions and recipes had little interest for her at the best of times; just now they had none.

Logan put down his manuscript, got to his feet, and strolled to join her at the window. With his hands in his pockets, he scanned the blowing snow and oppressive, low-hanging clouds. He glanced at her, then looked away again.

"Is it really that much of a marvel, or are you sulking?"

"I enjoy watching it," Clare answered briefly.

"I wouldn't have taken you for a nature lover."

"No, but then, you know nothing about me." She could not get used to that mocking inflection, especially knowing how little she deserved it.

"True."

Clare slanted him a glance from the corner of her eyes. The fact that he had crossed the room to speak to her could be looked on as a concession, she supposed. Regardless of the provocation he had given her, it was ungracious of her to snap at him. The least she could do was to meet him halfway. "You mentioned last night that you were used to the cold weather. Does that mean that you have spent a lot of time here in the winter, or simply that you have grown used to it in the last few days?"

"This is one of my favorite places, all right, for obvious reasons," he said, "but I also come here for the skiing. I enjoy cold-weather sports. I guess if I hadn't been an actor, I would have wound up a ski bum."

Without meaning to, Clare found herself smiling. "Then all this," she said, waving toward the flying snow, "should be good news to you."

"I will admit it has its attractions, but I think the best thing about a fresh snowfall, especially one like this, is that it covers all trace of other human beings. There may be beer cans, candy wrappers, and foil from cigarette packages under the snow, but at least you can't see them. When the snow stops and you walk out into the woods, everything is clean and quiet. If you are lucky, the only footprints are your own. There is a hush that comes then that is unlike any other time, and the air is so pure and cold, it rings in your lungs. It's as if you are the only thing alive, the beginning and end of creation, the center of the universe, and yet an unmistakable part of all that is natural around you."

His voice was quiet, reflective, but it was plain that what he said held special meaning for him. "There are not many places where that is possible anymore," Clare commented. "Something always spoils it. In the South it is the scars of timber cutting or the smoke from some factory."

"Here it's the things I mentioned, or the racket of a snowmobile."

"The whine of a chain saw . . . or a hunter's shot."

"Or the litter of their shell casings. Things like that are why I support the formation of wilderness areas — unspoiled places without logging roads, or even trails, closed to any kind of mechanized travel, to logging or hunting, areas left to go back to the wild. These places will be so remote, only people who care about meeting nature on its own terms will want to make the effort to hike back into them. But at least for that breed the opportunity will be there. If we go on as we are now, the generations to come will never know what that means, because the few places like that left will be gone."

"I thought the secretary of agriculture recently recommended that several million acres be set aside for designation as wilderness sections."

"He did, but already the special-interest groups, the lumber and tourism industries and the sports organizations, are screaming and mounting a campaign of advertising against it. The only thing for those of us who oppose the special-interest groups is to scream louder."

"It does seem as if I remember seeing you on some program concerned with conservation."

"I speak my piece when I think it will do any good. One of the few advantages I have found to being a big Hollywood name is the extra weight it gives you when you decide to throw yourself behind something."

"I would not have thought you had much time for such things."

"I don't have nearly enough. That is why I would like to make the conservation issue the theme of my next picture."

"A propaganda film?" Clare queried lightly.

"You could call it that, though it is also a historical drama with, I think, a balanced presentation of the arguments for progress and free enterprise, as well as for my own views."

He went on to tell her the story line of what emerged as a tale filled with grandeur and passion, fine characters and stirring events. If allowed to unfold against the color and majesty of the mountains, it would be a picture of epic proportions and great visual impact.

"It sounds marvelous," Clare said when he had finished. "Will you start on it soon?"

55

"I'm not sure. I still have to sell the idea, or the screenplay, to the producer I want to put it on film."

"You mean you found this screenplay, or book, or whatever it is yourself?"

" 'Found' is not exactly the right word. It may help you to understand my enthusiasm for the story if I tell you I wrote it."

Clare swung around to stare at him, her gray eyes startled. "You?"

"Is that so unbelievable?"

"No, not really. It's just that it seems strange."

"In what way?"

"People who develop one talent are usually inclined to stop there. A great many actors become directors, but that is really an extension of a craft they already know, isn't it? Writing is something entirely different."

"It has always seemed to me that writers must have a good ear for dialogue and a sense of how people act and react in any given situation. They have to understand movement and emotion and all the other small details that make a character believable."

"You may be right," Clare agreed, "though I am not in a position to say, since I concentrate on nonfiction. But I can't believe people aren't falling over themselves to produce this film,

your screenplay, to see if you could persuade me to write a little propaganda in support of your cause?"

"No," he answered, his voice hard and his blue gaze meeting her eyes squarely. "The fact is, I had forgotten what you are until after I had begun to discuss it with you. However, I feel sure that if I tell you everything I said about it is off the record, I can depend upon you to honor the request, and keep it that way."

Clare lifted her chin. Goaded by his lack of belief, she said, "You may think you can, but you can't be sure."

"No," he answered, his voice grim once more, "I can't, can I?"

3

The remainder of the day passed much more quickly than Clare had expected. She spent the better part of it huddled into a blanket on a chair beneath one of the windows, reading the manuscript of Logan's screenplay in the gray light that fell through the opening. Lunch was a sketchy affair of bread and cold meat washed down with canned juice, icy cold straight from the kitchen cabinet. Afterward, Logan was restless, prowling through the house, checking the water lines to see if they had begun to freeze, draining the hot-water tank against the possibility of its bursting as the water inside turned to ice. This water he set before the fire in every available bucket, pot, and dishpan in preparation for their baths later that night. When that was done, he returned to his place before the hearth, but it was not long before he was on his feet again, dragging on his jacket and gloves, pulling on his cap.

Clare looked up in time to see him step through the sliding doors out onto the deck. She frowned a little as his tall shape disappeared into the swirling cloud of snow; then she returned to her reading.

Sometime later, a glowing log in the fireplace burned in two and fell into the glowing coals with a crackling flare of red-orange sparks. The sound broke Clare's absorption. She looked up, assailed by a sudden sense of alarm. Logan had not returned.

Tragic tales she had heard of people lost in snowstorms, dying within a few yards of warmth and safety, flashed through her mind. Setting the bound manuscript aside, she threw back the blanket and stood up, moving quickly to the glass door. She pulled it open, letting a cold rush of snow-laden air sweep into the room. She could see nothing beyond the swift-falling white flakes. Hesitating only a moment, she stepped out onto the deck, kicking through drifted snow reaching well above her ankles. The wind caught at her, tossing the long strands of her hair in wild abandon, stinging her face with cold particles of ice, and flapping her coat about her knees.

"Logan?" she called.

Her voice was caught by the wind and thrown back at her with a muffled and weak sound. There was no answer.

"Logan!" she cried again, fear rising inside her as she thought of how long the blond actor had been out in such inhospitable weather conditions. Struggling to the balcony railing, she leaned over it, dislodging the heaped snow that lined it, so that it fell like a tiny avalanche.

"Logan!"

"What is it?"

The question came from directly behind her.

She swung around so quickly in the soft drifts that she stumbled and might have fallen if Logan had not caught her. The hard strength of his hands bit into her forearms, steadying her. Weak with relief, she let herself rest against his chest. An instant later, she stepped back, pushing her trembling hands deep into her coat pocket.

"Where were you?" she demanded.

"I had just come in at the side door when I heard you shouting. What is wrong?"

His outdoor clothing coated with snow and the flakes that glistened on the ends of his lashes and on the gold stubble of his beard were evidence of the truth of what he said. "Nothing. Nothing is wrong. It just seemed like you had been gone a long time."

"Did you think I had run out on you? Even if the idea crossed my mind, I wouldn't get far in this. I just went out for a breath of fresh air, and I can tell you this much: there is plenty of it out here to be had."

"I can believe it," Clare said, smiling even as she shivered.

"There is also more than a little inside the house now. Did you know you left the door open? We'll be lucky if we don't have to get out the snow shovel to clear a path to the fire."

"Oh, no," Clare exclaimed, "all our lovely warmth, and the carpet will be soaked." In the concern of the moment Clare was able to cover her confusion, to turn back into the house with a creditable attempt at nonchalance. She bent to shake the blown snow from the mat, then stamped her boots to free them of caked chunks.

Logan removed his gloves, then dragged off his cap and began to swat himself free of the clinging ice particles. When he was reasonably dry, he raked his fingers through his hair and began to remove his jacket. His gaze on Clare, he spoke her name, giving it a deep, clear sound.

She looked up, her gray eyes dark.

"I do appreciate the thought," he said, and smiled, a slow curving of the lips without mockery or guile, though in its warmth there was a suspended, measuring quality. It lasted no more than an instant before he turned away. "Did you ever make snow ice cream?" he asked. "You use milk, sugar, and vanilla flavoring mixed into some of that white stuff falling out there. All at once I have this terrible craving for it. Want to give it a try?"

Whether from the need to keep warm, or from the sheer lack of anything else to occupy their minds, food began to take on an exaggerated importance. Their appetites grew ravenous. Scarcely an hour after the snow ice cream had been demolished, they were searching in the cabinets for canned soup and beans, looking for aluminum foil to wrap around potatoes to bake in the coals, and trying to rig some way of grilling a steak. In the end, they pan-broiled the meat in butter. It was charred black on the outside and pink on the inside; still, it was the most delectable thing Clare had ever eaten. They laughed at each other as they tried to cut the steak without mangling their paper plates or destroying the surface of the coffee table, and with extreme politeness, and secret hungry longing, each insisted that the other eat the last potato, ending finally by dividing it between them. And then, when the dishes had been washed in some of the water Logan had been heating all afternoon, they stretched out facedown on the cushions before the fire and discussed the possibility of popping corn, using the short-handled pots in the kitchen.

Taking advantage of the amazing ease between them, Clare mentioned the screenplay. She had finished reading it just before dinner. The feeling of pleasure and uplift that the story had given her was so strong that she had wanted to congratulate him at once. She had refrained only because she had been afraid he would find her compliments suspect. Now, with her enthusiasm tempered by the wait, she could discuss it more objectively.

The story line concerned two brothers, both hard and strong-willed, who travel west in the middle of the nineteenth century to make a new life for themselves, and eventually come into conflict over the way they perceive people, the land, and its valuable resources. The characters of the two men and their relationship with each other were fascinating, but to Clare the roles of the women who loved them lacked depth. They were too superficial, too concerned with themselves to have generated the emotions directed toward them, or to have withstood the dangers and hardships they had to face.

Logan, to give him his due, listened to her ideas, though it was plain that he did not agree with them. His attitude was annoying, but Clare did not press the argument. The problem was a minor flaw in what she was inclined to think would be a tremendous motion picture. Certainly it was not worth endangering the tenuous peace that reigned between them. Why should she risk it for something that within a few hours, when the snowstorm had blown itself out, would have nothing whatever to do with her?

Sighing a little, Clare raised herself to a sitting position and pushed up the sleeves of her sweater, rubbing at her wrists.

"You have been doing that all evening," Logan observed. "Is something the matter?"

"I suppose it's just that I'm not used to the dry air, or wearing wool for any length of time. The ribbing on this sweater is irritating my skin."

"It can't be very comfortable."

She had to agree. As if her words confirmed something he had suspected, Logan pushed to his feet and left the room. He returned shortly, carrying one of his shirts.

"Here," he said, tossing it down beside her. "Maybe this will be better."

It felt better, there could be no doubt about

that; what it looked like was another thing entirely. Clare, staring at herself in the bathroom mirror by the glow of the flashlight standing on its end, let a grin twitch across her lips. The shirt of soft cotton flannel had all the flattering fit of a hospital gown. The shoulder seams hung halfway down her arms, the cuffs of the sleeves flapped below her hands, and the tail of it struck her not far above the knees. In addition, the color of the plaid was a brilliant blue, red, and black, a terrible clash with the soft green of her skirt.

And then, as she stared at herself, a peculiar feeling moved over her. It lasted for no more than a flicker of time before she gave a hard shake of her head and began to roll up the sleeves with a quick carelessness. So she was wearing Logan Longcross's shirt? That was no excuse for going into an adolescent daze. He was just an actor, a man — one, she must admit, who was turning out to be more reasonable about her presence than she had expected. She would spend one more night here with him. By tomorrow the snow would have stopped and she would carry on with her plans. By this time the next day, she and Beverly would be laughing over the whole episode, and that would be the end of it. It was strange that the prospect did not make her feel like smiling now.

Clare woke to silence. She lay staring up at the beams of the cathedral ceiling for long moments before she recognized what was wrong. The wind had dropped, and the strange brightness that filled the room meant that beyond the draperies drawn over the windows the blizzard was over and the sun was shining. Instinctively Clare turned toward the other bed. It was empty. Logan had gone out already. His jacket, gloves, and cap were gone from where he had left them the evening before.

Throwing back the cover, Clare sat up and pulled on her boots. When she had gained her feet, she unfastened her skirt and tucked the excess material of Logan's shirt into the waistband before buttoning it up again. She felt crumpled, and more than a little weary of the clothes she was wearing. She could do nothing about that, but she could bring some sort of order to the wild tangle of her hair.

With the hairbrush from her tote in one hand and a tortoiseshell hair clip in the other, Clare moved from one window to the other, staring out, entranced. The snow covered everything like a thick layer of spun-sugar icing. Upon its diamondlike surface, the sun sparkled with dazzling brilliance. The pine, spruce, and fir trees near the house stood with their branches weighted with snow, like flocked Christmas trees, their lower limbs half-buried in the smothering whiteness. In the front of the house, toward the road, Clare saw the deep tracks Logan had made as he left from the side door and tramped away over the virgin snowfall. Where he could have gone, she had no idea, though the trail he had left seemed to lead down the snow-covered roadway.

The rear of the chalet, with its glass doors, its expanse of windows reaching up to the roof-line and down to the outside deck, held the greatest surprise. It overlooked a steep, walled canyon with evergreens clinging to its side and blue shadows at the bottom. On the far side, the trees were silvered with their burden of snow, and beyond them lay a range of blue mountains frosted white against the cerulean of the sky. It was a stunning view. Clare stood looking out over it for a long time, her gray eyes thoughtful. Then, with an abrupt movement she turned away, fastened the clip over her smooth hair at the nape of her neck, and went briskly about the business of cooking breakfast.

She was cracking eggs into the pan where she had fried bacon when Logan came through the door from the laundry. He threw down the burden he carried and took a deep breath. "I could smell the bacon and coffee a hundred yards away," he said.

Her attention on what she was doing, Clare said over her shoulder, "I suppose you are hungry again?"

"Starving."

"It will only be a minute." She turned to smile, then let her glance drop to the bundle at his feet. It was an instant before recognition came. "My suitcase!"

"You said so little about having to wear the same clothes for two days that I thought you deserved a reward."

"Oh, Logan. You shouldn't have done it, but I'm so glad you did. I don't know how to thank you."

"Slip another egg into the pan there, that's a good girl," he answered, and picked up the bag to carry it up the spiral stairs to one of the bedrooms for her.

It was after breakfast before Clare could turn her attention to a change of clothing. Shutting herself up in the frigid bedroom, she replaced what she was wearing from the skin out, mourning only that she could not take a long hot bath before donning the fresh clothing. She could have done so, if she had only waited a little while, she discovered. The first thing she noticed when she emerged from the bedroom in jeans, a knit shirt, and a chunky pullover sweater was the Tiffany light burning brightly over the table.

"The power is back on!" she said as she carried Logan's shirt through to the laundry.

"It came on about five minutes ago. That means the snowplows are out on the main roads. They should get here by this afternoon."

"That's good. Beverly, the friend I was going to stay with, will be standing on her head. It wouldn't surprise me to find out she had called in the police to locate me."

"I suspect most of the roads into this area have been closed since dark day before yesterday. People up here make allowances for this sort of thing. Your friend probably has a good idea that something like this happened. I doubt she will do anything drastic unless you don't show up a few hours after the roads are cleared."

Clare nodded. "You may be right."

"Since there is nothing we can do until the roads are open, and as long as you are warmly dressed, what do you say to a walk?"

"I would love it," Clare said, brightening; then her expression grew doubtful. "But you have already been out this morning. Are you sure you want to go again?"

"I'm sure. Besides, I have something to show you."

They set out immediately, both of them well wrapped up, including caps and gloves, with the addition, for Clare, of a brilliant red muffler over her camel's hair coat. It was not difficult to decide where they were going. They turned in the same direction Logan had taken that morning, following the path he had made in the snow. It could lead only one place, to her car on the side of the embankment.

Rather than beat a trail of her own, Clare followed along in Logan's footsteps, her view blocked by his broad shoulders. It was not until they reached the place where she had gone over the edge that she could look down and see where her car had come to stop.

The sight brought her to an abrupt halt. With her hands clenched and her face pale, she stared downward. Here the road paralleled the same canyon that Logan's house overlooked. It had the same evergreens, the same perpendicular walls. Only the great trunk of the huge ponderosa pine had kept Clare's car from plunging, rolling over and over, bounding off snowcovered rocks to the blue-shadowed bottom a thousand feet below.

Slowly Clare lifted her gray eyes to stare at Logan.

"Yes," he said softly. "It was quite a chance you took, wasn't it?"

"I didn't know it was like that," she whispered.

"I don't doubt it."

"No, but you still think I drove off the road deliberately. You must be crazy if you think I would risk so much just for an interview, no matter who it was with."

His eyes narrowed. "Where was the risk, if you didn't know what this drop-off was like? If it had been no more than a steep shoulder there would have been no danger, just a lady in distress with her car out of commission. As it turned out, the excuse was even better, a perfect alibi, because who could possibly believe anybody would do such a stupid thing as drive over the side of that on purpose?"

Without a word, Clare swung away from him. There was fury in every line of her body as she marched back the way she had come. She neither hesitated nor turned back when he called her name.

Now that she was out, Clare had no intention of returning to the confinement of the house. The air was still crisp and cold, but it was also invigoratingly fresh. Past the house, the going was harder, since she had to make her own trail. She was soon panting for breath in the rarefied atmosphere, but she no longer felt the cold. As she penetrated deeper into the woods, a soft quiet descended. She was alone. Around her lay the thick mantle of snow, disturbed only by her footsteps. The clean sharp smell of the evergreens hung in the air. As she brushed against their branches, the fine snow shifted down, falling without sound. On impulse, she scooped a handful from a spruce bough and touched it to her tongue. It tasted like the air, fresh and cold and faintly resinous.

Moving more slowly now, she wandered on. The only sound was the crunch of snow beneath her boots. Nothing moved. There was no wind, no animals, no birds, nothing to mar the perfect stillness. And then, at the foot of a great granite boulder capped with snow, she found where movement had been frozen. It was a small deep spring. Its slow-running waters had turned to ice, sheathing its rock channel in sculptured turns and molding icicles where it poured over the rocks, building them in layers, so that they hung like stalactites in an underground cavern. The sun striking through the trees glittered on the hoarfrost that sheeted it with the shimmer of finest crystal.

Clare felt the constriction around her heart ease. Taking a deep breath, she let it out in slow pleasure, aware with a sense of wonder that this, this instant of timeless beauty, was what Logan had been trying to describe to her. If the great destroyer, man, came to claim this spot he would cut down the trees, capture the spring water in nice, useful concrete fittings, fill the air with the smell of gasoline exhaust, and shatter the quiet with the noise of machines. So much of the earth had been subjected to that kind of civilization. Why couldn't a few such places as this be left?

Behind her came the sound of a cold-stiffened limb brushing against cloth. She turned, to see Logan standing a short distance away.

"Sorry," he said, the single word carrying easily in the intense quiet.

His apology was not for what he had said, but for following her, for disturbing her reverie.

"It doesn't matter" she answered.

As if released by her words, he came closer. She watched him from the corners of her eyes, determination growing with every step he took. He had not been overly concerned with her feelings. Why should she trouble herself with his?

"There is something I have been wanting to ask you," she said, her voice reflective. "Since this is all off the record, I may as well. Does

Janine Hobbs have anything to do with the hitch in having her husband produce your screenplay?"

"What do you know about Janine Hobbs?"

"Only what I read in the papers," she quipped. "I am a fair hand at putting two and two together."

"I can imagine," he answered, his voice hard.

"Are you going to tell me?"

"Why not? The more you know, the more frustrating it will be that you can't use it." He sent her a mocking smile, one that she mimicked perfectly in return.

Clare thought real amusement quirked his mouth before he looked quickly away, but she could not be sure. "Well?" she inquired.

"I am trying to decide how to tell you this without having you accuse me of conceit again," he answered. "Mrs. Marvin Hobbs has more time on her hands than she can fill. At a guess, I would say she is about my age, give or take a year, one of your California women who was once an actress before she decided marriage to a producer was a more lucrative career. She was never a particularly great talent, but she likes to think that if it had not been for Marvin, she could have been. She makes it a point to polish her image now, to keep herself in shape so she can compare favorably with all the attractive young females that show up at parties in L.A. She swims, she jogs, she plays golf, she skis, spends five hours a week in the beauty salon, five with her masseuse, and two weeks out of every year on a beauty farm. She is susceptible to flattery, and it is not exactly unknown for young actors on the way up to try to get her attention first in order to bring themselves to the notice of her husband."

"Good grief," Clare said, as much in wonder for Logan's analysis of the woman's failings as for the picture of her he had drawn.

He gave a small nod. "Janine has become so used to that kind of notice that she expects it. If it isn't forthcoming, she is apt to take it as a personal insult. It doesn't matter that she doesn't feel a thing for any of the men; the main thing is the feeling they give her that she is desirable and important. The worst of it is, she *is* important. Because of her experience in the business and a certain knack for recognizing star quality, or popular properties, Marvin listens to her. Janine knows it and uses it to her advantage."

When he did not go on, Clare said, "That is a harsh judgment."

"Maybe so, but that doesn't make it any less accurate."

"It doesn't say much for the men who use her, either."

77

He glanced at her, a hard light in his blue eyes. "You think I'm one of those men? Forget it. I have never been so desperate for a job that I would go after one that way. That is part of the problem, I think. I am only guessing, but I would say that the fact I never seek her out, seldom speak to her except out of courtesy, has had something to do with her overwhelming interest in me lately."

"Aha," Clare said, "I begin to see. She is infatuated with you. Is that it?"

"I don't know that I would put it just that way, but that's basically right."

"Then I fail to see your problem."

"Is that so?" Logan said grimly. "Then let me explain it to you. The woman thinks she is in love with me. That being so, she is a little irritated at my lack of response. The last few weeks before I left California, she came out to the house where I was staying a half-dozen times, crying and complaining about the way Marvin neglects her. She showed up on the set of the movie I just finished shooting so often the director threatened to quit. Any other time, I could have handled it; even women like Janine Hobbs understand plain language. As it was, I had already approached her husband about my screenplay. He was interested, but not ready to commit himself. Janine was present when the discussion first came up. She knew how committed I was to the project, how much I wanted Marvin in on it. She let me understand, very carefully, of course, that if I didn't play up to her, she would be so disappointed she could not be responsible for what she might say to her husband about the feasibility of doing my script."

"I suppose you pointed out to her that it just might make her husband a teeny bit angry if he should discover the two of you were more friendly than you should be?"

"I did. She told me that Marvin had been hearing such things for years, and that he knew exactly how much faith to put in gossip circulating around the movie capital."

"Dear me," Clare said cheerfully. "You were in a bind! The lady to ruin your chances if you didn't do as she said, the husband just as likely to ruin them if you did."

"That's about the size of it. If I hadn't thought support of the wilderness areas in this country was worth the cost, I would have said to the devil with the whole thing."

"So you did the next best thing," Clare suggested. "You got out of town."

"The reason for that goes just a bit further, though what you say is more or less true. We had completed the movie I was working on, a Hobbs production. There was a party for the cast and crew. Marvin came by for a time, then went on back to his office. Janine stayed on. Not long after her husband left, Janine complained of feeling sick and asked me to take her home. Before we had gone a half-dozen blocks, she miraculously recovered. A drink, she said, was all that she needed."

"And you believed her," Clare said, shaking her head in a pretense of sorrow for such credulity.

He sent her a quelling look. "We went into the club Janine pointed out, a quiet-enough place. And then along came a photographer. A simple picture would have been fine; it would have shown nothing more than two friends having a drink. But Janine's timing was bad. She chose that moment to throw herself into my arms. When the flash went off, she started crying hysterically." He shrugged. "I am afraid I lost my temper."

"Yes, I know. You slugged the poor man, just a working photographer out trying to turn an honest dollar."

"If you think so, you are more innocent than you have any right to be," he said, a glint in his blue eyes. "But that wasn't the end of it. When Janine stopped crying, she said she no longer cared whether her husband knew about our 'affair' or not; she wanted him to know about it. It's a miracle I didn't strangle her right there.

Instead, I tried to talk to her. She jumped to the conclusion that the reason I wasn't interested was that there was another woman. There wasn't, but it seemed as good an explanation as any, so long as Janine was willing to accept it without being insulted. It was better than telling her to her face that she just didn't appeal to me. I should have known better. She began to hound me for details. I stood it for three days; then it was either get away from her or say something I would regret. I came up here."

"You can't stay here forever," Clare said, raking a smooth spot in the snow with the toe of her boot.

"No," he said, "but I am hoping that by the time I have to go back to the coast, Janine will have found somebody else."

"If you really think she will, I suppose I will have to acquit you of conceit," Clare said, slanting him a quick glance. "What will you do if she doesn't?"

"I'll have to find myself another producer, won't I? Marvin Hobbs may be the best; that doesn't mean he is the only one."

Clare gave a slow nod. "I . . . I hope you make your picture. It would be a pity if no one ever saw it."

He looked down at her, an arrested expression in the clear blue of his eyes as he surveyed the delicate arch of her brows, the firm set of her chin, and the tender curls escaping from the clip that held back her hair. He looked away again. "I expect we had better be getting back," he said, his voice-flat.

They had a quick lunch of soup and a sandwich, sitting in stiff formality at the table. Afterward they cleared away the dishes, then scrubbed the frying pan and pots they had been using in the coals of the fireplace, making short work of the job with the now plentiful supply of hot water. The blankets were folded and put away, the sheets placed in the laundry, and the cushions settled back on the couch. Clare and Logan worked silently. In little more than an hour all trace of the hours they had spent cooped up in that one room had been removed. As soon as the road was clear, Logan would take her into town, where she could call Beverly, and at the same time, a garage to tow her car into town for repairs. If Beverly was able to come and take her back to their cabin, then that would be that. If not, Logan had offered to drive her to Beverly's cabin himself. Clare would just as soon it did not come to that: the sooner she was able to put this episode behind her, the better it would be.

She was in the upstairs bedroom putting the last of her things in her suitcase when she heard the grinding of gears and the roar of a straining engine. That would be the snowplow, she thought. She snapped the latches of her suitcase shut and looked around for her coat. Logan would be ready to go almost at once. He had gone outside sometime ago to clear the drive so he could get his car out of the closed garage at the back of the house.

Finding her coat, Clare slipped it on. Her tote bag lay beside it, and she slung the strap over her shoulder before turning to pick up her suitcase.

She had reached the stairs and started down before she realized the snowplow, if that was what it was, had stopped in front of the chalet. Quiet fell as the engine was switched off. There came the sound of an automobile door closing, followed by the crunch of footsteps moving toward the front door. Frowning a little, Clare continued down the spiral staircase, coming to a halt at the bottom. A slight sound from the direction of the kitchen drew her attention. Logan stood there, still in his boots and jacket, a water glass in his hand. His expression was withdrawn as he met her eyes across the room. As the front doorbell pealed, he set the glass on the cabinet and moved with deliberation to answer it.

The man who stood outside on the deck was not large, and yet, with his burly shape, his craggy features and commanding attitude, he gave the impression of being a big man. From his steely-gray hair and the lines in his tanned face, he appeared to be in his early fifties. He wore an overcoat hanging open to reveal a business suit of conservative cut and color.

"Logan," he said with a curt inclination of his head. "Mind if I come in?"

Logan swung the door wider and stepped back. The man gave a perfunctory scrape to his shoes on the doormat, then stepped inside, striding farther into the room as Logan pushed the door to behind him. "Have a seat," Logan directed.

"I'd rather stand," the man replied, his voice hard. "My business won't take long. I think you know why I am here."

"I don't believe I do," Logan answered, a softly dangerous inflection threading his tone, "any more than I know how you found me."

"Finding people is not hard, if you know the right person to ask. All I had to do was mention to your agent that I was anxious to talk to you. For some reason he was certain you wouldn't mind being interrupted; he seemed to think you would be alone, something we both know isn't true."

"That's right, Marvin. I'm not alone," Logan answered, ignoring the heavy sarcasm directed at him, and also the edging of menace in the producer's tone. "There is someone here with me you should meet."

"I am well aware," the man began angrily, swinging to keep Logan in view as he moved toward the spiral staircase. At the sight of Clare, he stopped in mid-sentence. The blank look of surprise on his face was so obvious it came near to being comical.

"Clare," Logan said, touching his fingers to her elbow to lead her forward. "This is Marvin Hobbs. Marvin, Clare Thornton."

Hobbs recovered quickly. "How do you do?" he said, his eyes moving from Clare to Logan and then to the suitcase behind her. Ignoring her civil greeting, he went on. "Are you leaving, or just arriving?"

"Leaving," Clare answered.

"Then you must have been caught here by the blizzard?"

Clare flung a quick questioning glance at Logan. If he saw it, he gave no sign. "Yes," she said finally.

"And I suppose you were alone, you and Logan?"

"That's right," Clare said, twin spots of anger beginning to burn on her cheekbones.

Amazingly, a crooked smile moved over Marvin Hobbs' mouth. "I see," he said, a knowing, satisfied sound in his voice.

"No," Logan corrected him quietly, "I don't

think you do. Clare is my fiancée."

Clare swung her head to stare at Logan. His face was closed and unreadable.

The older man cleared his throat, the dull flush of a decent man caught in the wrong rising under his skin. "I didn't . . . I must congratulate you then, and apologize, doubly. You will have to admit I had cause for my error."

Marvin Hobbs had expected to find his wife with Logan; there could be little doubt of that. His words could apply to his misjudgment of the situation between Logan and Clare, but they could just as easily mean he thought he had been given reason to believe Janine would be there. Clare was not surprised that Logan refused to commit himself by agreeing or disagreeing with the man. As for Logan's announcement, it was not every day that she received the honorary title of fiancée. Though the shock of it still tingled along her veins, she was not so stupid as to think Logan meant anything except to save her embarrassment and to put any suspicions Hobbs might have completely to rout. It appeared to have served the purpose, but if Logan was not going to undo what he had accomplished, he must begin to yield a little.

In defiance of the tension between the two men, Clare said, "It doesn't matter, Mr. Hobbs. I believe you drove here, didn't you? Could you tell us what the roads are like?"

"Anxious to get away, are you?"

"Not at all," Clare said, aware even as she searched her mind for an excuse that would blend with what he had been told that she was not cut out for this kind of subterfuge. "It is only that I . . . I don't want to distract Logan from his work."

"I don't imagine he minds," Hobbs said. "But what work is this, Logan? I thought you had finished this screenplay of yours?"

"So did I, but Clare seems to think that certain characters, most of them female, need to be a bit stronger."

"Does she, now? She may be right, but I hope you don't intend to make any major changes. I like the script the way it is. As a matter of fact, I think it would be a good idea for us to get down to some serious discussion about it." He turned back to Clare. "Are you staying in Aspen, Miss Thornton?"

"Not in Aspen, but in the area."

"Good. I want you and Logan to have dinner with me tonight. I owe you that much for barging in here, and it will be as good a time as any for seeing what terms we can come up with on this new production."

Once again Clare glanced at Logan. The look on his face was far from helpful as he stood watching her, with one arm resting on the newel post and something perilously like laughter lurking at the back of his eyes.

Clare turned to the other man. "It is kind of you to include me in the invitation, Mr Hobbs," she said finally. "However, I am sure you and Logan can get along much better if I am not there."

"I don't know about that. It seems to me you may be a young lady with something worth contributing."

"No, really, I would rather not."

"Logan, I leave it to you to persuade her," Marvin Hobbs said. "I am sure you can do a much better job than I can. I will reserve a table for seven o'clock in the dining room of my hotel. I hired a four-wheel-drive vehicle to get up here, but I don't see why you can't make it out with street tires and chains, after the plow comes. I'm looking forward to seeing both of you at seven."

Furnishing them with the name and address of the place where he was staying, the producer shook hands with Logan, nodded to Clare, and took his leave.

4

"I don't suppose he will be too disappointed when I don't show up," Clare said when the sound of the four-wheel vehicle had faded in the distance.

"I think he will," Logan answered. "He is still not sure you are real."

A small smile curved her mouth. "He's right, I'm not."

"You could be."

The suggestion was tentative, as though he was trying the taste and feel of it himself. Clare tilted her head. "Off the record, of course," she said dryly, "and only long enough to convince Marvin Hobbs that you have no designs on his wife?"

"Something like that," he agreed, his gold-tipped lashes shielding his expression. "Don't tell me you wouldn't like to know how the meeting turns out?"

She stared at him. "Of course I would, but I can't believe you would be willing to have me there."

"Yes, it's strange how things work out, isn't it?"

His tone was much too bland. Her gray eyes narrowed in suspicion, she said, "Aren't you afraid I might take advantage of the situation? If you acknowledge me in public as your fiancée, things could get sticky."

He lifted an eyebrow. "They might, but I think you are too intelligent for that."

"Intelligent instead of ethical? I like that!"

"I thought you would," he murmured.

Clare chewed the inside of her lip. Did he really want her to come, or was he making the suggestion only to see what she would say? She did not think for a moment that he needed to hide behind the fiction of a fiancée, despite his offer. What she should do was firmly refuse to have anything to do with it. That would show him she had no designs on him, either as a fan or as a writer of newspaper articles. But wait — was that by any chance his purpose in encouraging her, to find out once and for all the truth of what she had told him about herself? If she was what she had said, an amateur free-lance writer who had stumbled upon his retreat by accident, then she must refuse. But if she were an experienced professional out for a big story, then she would not dare let such an opportunity as this slip through her fingers.

"What's it going to be?" he inquired, his smile just a shade too knowing for her liking.

"You really expect me to jump at this chance, don't you?" she said with a lift of her chin. "You have it all figured out, because you never believed what I said in the first place. Well, Logan Longcross, as much pleasure as it would give me to prove you wrong, I think I would prefer to confuse you instead. Has it occurred to you that if I wanted to go out of my way to convince you of my good faith and throw you off guard, I would refuse to play this role you have written for me and hope to catch the juicy developments from the sidelines? As it is, I am going to do no such thing. I am going to accept Marvin Hobbs's invitation to dinner. Whether you wanted one or not, you have just acquired yourself a fiancée for the evening."

After some discussion, Clare and Logan decided the best thing to be done was to follow Hobbs into town as soon as possible. There they could take rooms at a hotel. From the way Logan spoke, Clare thought he meant to pay the cost of her room, since she would be staying, more or less, for his sake. She was just as determined to pay her own way, though she saw no point in making an issue of it just now.

From her room Clare could call Beverly, explain the delay and her plans for the evening, and arrange to meet her the following morning. Logan would take care of having her car retrieved, since he would be better able to give the garage tow truck directions to it. With that out of the way, he would have to go shopping. When he had packed for his stay at his mountain home, formal attire had not been one of the things he had thrown into his luggage. Though he had worn a suit for the flight into Aspen, the shirt with it had been open-necked in the European style. With a different shirt and a tie, it would serve the purpose. His purchases out of the way, they would be able to dress for dinner in comfort, and then, after dinner, Logan would not have to drive back out to his house over roads in uncertain condition. In addition, Clare would not have to ask Beverly and John to undertake the same trouble and risk.

The trouble could not be minimized. By the time Logan had zipped his clothing into a travel bag and carried it with Clare's suitcase out to the car, clouds had closed down over the tops of the mountains once more. Before they reached the main road toward Aspen, snow mixed with icy rain had begun to fall.

The town of Aspen was founded in 1879 by a group of men prospecting in the hills for silver. Originally called Ute City, it was renamed a few months later by B. Clark Wheeler, a promoter who helped to turn the collection of tents and log cabins into a boom town. Millions in silver were taken from the hillsides in the following decade; then, in 1893, silver was demonetized. The mines closed, but the Victorian town remained at eight thousand feet, high in the mountains, a perfect setting for a ski resort. The possibilities of the fine slopes and deep powder snow had not been lost on the miners. The first skis had been unloaded in Aspen in 1880. The sport only began to receive serious attention, however, just before World War II. It was not until long after the war, however, in 1957, that Aspen really began to come into its own.

This much of the background of the area Clare had been able to glean from the guidebook she had studied before she left home. Now, as she and Logan entered Aspen itself, she looked about her with interest. It was not a large town, but it was a pleasant one. The streets were wide and well-marked, the buildings a blend of nineteenth-century carpenter's Gothic, Swiss Alpine complete with Christmas motifs, and sharp-angled modern. Since all three styles favored the use of wood rather than masonry, they coexisted comfortably. Summer and winter visitors were the mainstay of the economy. Because of this it was not unnatural that most businesses were oriented toward their wants and needs. Specialty shops of all types abounded, from jewelry and glassware to ski rentals. In the center of town there was a shopping mall cobbled with brick and featuring small elegant shops with charming Victorian facades.

It was an experience walking into a hotel with Logan Longcross, something Clare intended to remember for a long time. Logan stepped out of the car and held the door for her. Glancing at the doorman, he smiled his slow smile. Immediately, heads turned, people appeared to take their bags, to park the car, to swing the heavy glass doors of the hotel open. A growing murmur of voices followed them to the desk in the lobby. The clerk behind the counter looked up, his frown a signal of the unlikelihood of their receiving a room without a reservation at that season. Looking again, he changed his mind. He even discovered, after a hurried consultation with the manager, that two rooms were available, one for Mr. Long-cross, one across the hall for his fiancée.

As they were closed into the elevator with a bemused bellhop clutching the handle of a luggage carrier, a pair of gray-haired matrons with wide eyes leaned with the closing door to catch the last possible glimpse of the actor. Clare glanced at Logan as they moved soundlessly upward, one brow lifted expressively. He grinned at her with a flash of white teeth and gave a slow shake of his head. "Sometimes it has its uses," he said.

In her room, Clare took off her coat, threw it with her tote bag into a chair, and moved to the telephone. She had no trouble getting through to Beverly. Her friend's rapturous greeting was quickly followed by a demand to know where she was and what had happened. Clare, leaning back against the headboard of the bed on which she was seated, told her.

"What did you say?"

Clare had to smile at the blank incomprehension in Beverly's voice. It was all she could do not to laugh aloud at the contrast to her first eager questions.

"I said, I wish I could see you tonight, but I promised to have dinner with Logan Long-cross."

"I thought that was what you said. Have

you gone stark, staring mad?"

"Not at all. I told you I had to take refuge from the snowstorm. Logan Longcross just happened to own the place that was closest to hand."

"You are joking, of course," Beverly said in resigned tones.

"Do you honestly think I would joke about such a thing, Beverly Hoffman?"

"I suppose not," Beverly conceded. "Still, I have the strangest feeling you haven't told me everything. Start at the beginning, and don't leave anything out."

"Couldn't it wait until in the morning?" Clare pleaded. "Logan will be coming back any minute, and I have to go and help him choose a shirt."

"You what!"

"You heard me. I'm not sure, but I think my job is to keep people at bay while he chooses it, but at any rate, I've told him I would be there. You will come and get me in the morning?"

"Yes, I will, though I'm not sure I'm not taking my life into my hands, having anything to do with such an affair. I don't suppose I could stand to stay away, though, not until I hear what you have got yourself into. Tell me the name of the hotel again."

Clare gave it to her, then apologized once

more for being such a laggard guest. They exchanged a few more words; then Clare, with a final good-bye, dropped the receiver into its cradle. With a faint smile still curving her mouth, she turned away. Beverly was a grand person. It was sweet of her to be so concerned and interested. The interest was inevitable, it seemed. Logan had not gotten where he was without being able to arouse the interest of women. Not that he tried. After the time they had spent together, she actually believed the attraction was a natural, unconscious force. She had been aware of it at first; then, as the hours had passed, she had come to see Logan not as an actor but as a man. With faults, yes, but also with ideals and a deep vein of sensitivity. Regardless of what Beverly might think, even in spite of the reasons she had given her own conscience, it was for the man and what he believed in, rather than for the actor, that she was here in this hotel room at this moment.

It came as no great surprise that the scene in the hotel lobby was repeated in the men's store where they went to replenish Logan's wardrobe. The sales clerk, a vision of sartorial splendor, seemed to think it was a specially conferred honor to be asked to help choose a shirt and tie to complement a dark blue suit. The combinations available appeared to be endless as the man snatched shirts from the shelves and folded ties artistically at their collars. He was only prevented from covering the counters with such ensembles by Logan, who held up a hand, pointed at a subdued yet distinctive set, and told the clerk to put it in a bag. If the price of the simple purchase made Clare blink, she was not alone. The crowd at their back, to judge from their whispers, were no more used to simple white tone-on-tone shirts and diagonal-stripe silk ties running to those figures than she was.

Autographs, the minute Logan's attention was free, were inevitable. With the ease of long practice, he managed to slash a few words and his signature on whatever was thrust at him, and keep moving at the same time. Clare, jostled and pushed by the growing crowd, saw herself being separated from him, until Logan reached out and caught her hand to draw it through the crook of his arm. He pressed it firmly against his side, and never stopped walking. Gamely smiling, ignoring the questions thrown at her, Clare was able to keep up with him as they passed through the swinging doors of the shop and out onto the street.

They were nearly through the gauntlet. The car was before them. Logan handed back the last immortalized paper bag and reached for the car's handle. At that moment there came a scream from across the street that sounded like his name. An automobile's brakes squealed, a horn blared, and then, as they turned, a woman dashed toward them across two lanes of traffic and flung herself into Logan's arms.

"Logan, darling! The things I do to get to you. Aren't you flattered?" She would have kissed him if he had not turned his head. As it was, her mouth brushed his cheek, leaving a smear of lip gloss.

"Janine, I didn't expect to see you here."

"No, I'm sure you didn't. Wasn't it clever of me to remember your passion for the mountains? You also mentioned skiing here at Aspen once or twice in my hearing. I have spent the past few days positively hounding the real-estate agents trying to discover whether you owned a condo or a house, without success. And then, just as I was about to give up and go meekly back to L.A., to the home and husband I deserted a week ago, I saw a man being trailed by a horde of women. Who else could it be, my darling Logan, except you?"

"I see."

"Not an enthusiastic welcome, I must say, but I will overlook it if you will come to dinner with me this evening at the lodge where I'm staying."

"Sorry, but my fiancée and I have made other plans."

"Your fiancée!"

"I haven't introduced you, have I? Clare, darling, this is Janine Hobbs, the wife of the man you met this morning. Janine, Clare. And, yes, you did hear right – we saw Marvin this morning. It is your husband we are dining with this evening."

Clare acknowledged her introduction with a quiet word. If it had not been for the scathing glance directed at her by Janine Hobbs earlier, relegating her to the status of one of the women trailing Logan, she might have felt sorry for the other woman. It would have been wasted pity. One minute she was pale beneath the golden, beautifully even tan of her skin, and her carefully made-up green eyes were wide with shock. The next, her color had returned and she was smoothing at the fur of the coat she wore with long, manicured fingers.

"Marvin is here?" the woman inquired, her tone nonchalant.

"The way I understand it, he flew in this morning."

"And went straight to where you were? His method of finding you was better than mine, it seems. He has always been good at twisting arms. But what was the hurry?"

Logan stared at her with narrowed eyes. "He seemed to think he might find you with me."

Janine shrugged. "I wonder where he could have gotten that idea."

"So do I," Logan answered.

"Oh, come, Logan, don't be so stuffy," Janine said, reaching out to touch his arm. "We both know very well what Marvin thought. I only wish it had been true. If it had not been for that terrible snowstorm —"

"Aren't you forgetting something?" Logan interrupted.

Clare, despite the fact that she had no real claim to consideration as a fiancée, was oddly grateful for the reminder of her presence. Janine Hobbs had not looked at her again after the brief startled glance when they had been introduced. Annoyance at the woman's familiarity with Logan and deliberate bad manners to herself rose within her. One hand was still caught in the crook of Logan's arm. Placing the other over it, Clare said, "I don't like to interrupt your conversation, darling ... but shouldn't we be going? We still have to dress for dinner, and we don't want to keep Mr. Hobbs waiting. Besides, we seem to be gathering an audience."

The last was true enough. The spectators, talking excitedly, had gathered seven and eight deep in a circle around them and were beginning to spill out into the street.

Logan sent a quick look around them. "Yes, I think you are right."

"Oh, what does it matter?" Janine exclaimed, fluffing her coat around her face, shaking back her fine, perfectly cut black hair. "Let them look."

Clare gave the other woman a pleasant smile. "There is always the possibility that one of the horde of women trying to get close to Logan will not be satisfied with looking. That kind of thing can get out of hand, you know, and I would just as soon he stayed in one piece. I don't intend to share him with anyone."

Janine's brow snapped together. "Are you suggesting I am one of the horde?"

"I wonder where you could have gotten that idea?" Clare, repeating Janine's mock-innocent phrase, could feel the tension in Logan's arm. She knew he had turned to look down at her, but she refused to meet his gaze.

Janine Hobbs looked from one to the other, anger hardening in her green eyes. "Don't let me keep you, then," she said. "I have an idea of the nature of your business with my husband, and how important it is to you."

There was an inflection in her voice Clare did not like, though Logan appeared not to hear it.

"We would invite you to join us this evening," he said, "but under the circumstances I doubt it would appeal to you."

Janine made no reply. The set of her face was cold, and her hands were clenched in the soft fur of her coat as she stood back so they could get into the car. As they drove away, she was still staring after them.

The distance back to the hotel was not long. Clare, staring through the windshield, spoke at once. "I am sorry if I embarrassed you."

"Amazed me, is more like it."

"I . . . it was nothing personal. I simply got tired of her pretending I didn't exist."

"I think she noticed you," he commented.

The ghost of a smile flickered across Clare's lips in response to his wry tone. "Do you think she will leave Aspen?"

"Somehow I doubt it," he answered, his voice tight and a frown between his eyes as he stared straight ahead.

Back in her room at the hotel, Clare ran a deep, hot bath and sprinkled a generous amount of rose-scented bath-oil beads into the water. She lay soaking in the silken luxury for a long time. At first she tried to hold her thoughts at bay, but they came crowding in. What had she let herself in for? She had been crazy to agree; the proof of it was her reluctance to explain her folly to Bev. She would make a fool of herself, be exposed as a fraud.

Surely there was some way she could get out of it? She could leave the hotel, call Bev to come and get her. Logan did not know who she was or where she lived, not really. There would be no recriminations.

There might also be no movie from Logan's script, and she would be to blame. Could she live with the guilt?

She must not think like that. She was making too much of what was no more than a dinner date. Nothing important would be decided. It would be a pleasant meal with a little business discussion over the coffee. When it was over, Logan would say good-bye and she would go on with her skiing vacation with a pleasant memory of an interesting encounter. What could be wrong with that? Nothing at all.

Why, then, did she have this feeling that she was getting into something she could not control? Could it possibly be because of her impulsive act this afternoon in laying claim to Logan? She could not imagine what had possessed her to do such a thing. Antagonism toward the other woman was one answer, but it was not completly satisfactory. What was even more puzzling was Logan's easy acceptance of her meddling, when she would have expected him to be furious. Perhaps he appreciated the reason for her interference and was glad of it? He had not said so, not in so many words, but neither had be objected. She would have to take that as a sign of encouragement, and go on as planned.

Clare had not expected to be going out much in the evening. She had only one outfit with her even remotely suitable for the type of formal dinner she expected to be attending. It was a lightweight sweater and matching floor-length skirt in a silky, lacelike knit. The top had a round, scalloped neck and draped sleeves that fell to the elbow. The hem of the skirt was scalloped also. Of a soft, dusty rose color, it also had ribbon trim around the neck and sleeves.

With so little choice, it did not take her long to dress. She had shampooed her hair in the tub and dried it with the hot-air drier she had brought with her in her suitcase. Now, to give herself a less casual look, she twisted the long blond length of it into a shining coil low on the nape of her neck and fastened it with gold-topped tortoiseshell pins. Simple hooped earrings and a flat serpentine chain of gold were her only jewelry. A little rose lip gel and a touch of mascara completed her makeup. By the time Logan came for her, she was not only ready but had been waiting for some time.

They had arranged to meet Marvin Hobbs in the lobby. He came forward to greet them as they stepped out of the elevator. Whether it was because of the producer's brusque manner, or the dispatch with which he led them into the dining room, they were not molested as they made their way to the corner table Hobbs had reserved for them.

The maître d' summoned a waiter and they ordered drinks. The opening amenities thus disposed of, the producer leaned back in his chair.

"I must say you make an attractive couple . . . remind me of Nordic royalty, with both of you so blond. Clare, you know you will make a lot of women jealous when this news gets out. For myself, I'm not sure it isn't Logan who should be envied."

"What a lovely compliment. Thank you," Clare replied.

For no reason that she could think of, there was a husky note in her voice. She looked away, staring around her at the restaurant's decor, the gingerbread ornamentation, the nineteenth-century wallpaper, and the intriguing collection of antiques mixed with luxuriant green plants that sat here and there. A pleasant buzz of conversation and tinkling china and glassware filled the air. Some few of the other diners were formally dressed, but the vast majority were in casual wear. Her gaze passed over and returned to a woman who stood in the doorway on the far side of the room. She wore a gown of shimmering silver mesh that glittered with her every movement, while a silver-fox cape hung from her shoulders. Her dark hair, partially covered by a small, close-fitting turban of the same mesh as her gown, gave her the look of a Parisian, except that no Frenchwoman would have dressed quite so obviously to attract attention.

Confident that she had achieved her object, the woman spoke to the maître d', who moved to greet her, then turned in their direction. Her red lips wearing a pouting smile, she started toward their table. It was Janine Hobbs.

"Marvin, darling! How marvelous to see you. I am so glad you could get away. When I met Logan this afternoon and he told me you were here, I could not believe it. I never dreamed you would even think of joining me, or I would have let you know where I was staying."

The producer's back had been to the door. The expression on his face was carefully controlled as he swung to face his wife, then got to his feet. "My dear Janine, this is an unexpected pleasure."

"Is it? You mean Logan didn't tell you he had seen me? Perhaps I should not have accepted his invitation to dinner with you this evening, then?"

The look in her face was puzzled and faintly hurt. Her words conveyed the impression that there had been something not quite above-board in her meeting with Logan, as if he had been meddling in the affairs of husband and wife for his own ends, or else there had been a mix-up due to the hurried and clandestine nature of the communication between the two.

"Nonsense. Logan and Clare have only just arrived; we haven't had time to talk." Hobbs, his smile grim, held a chair for his wife. "I assume you have met Clare," he went on when he regained his seat.

Janine sent Clare a flickering smile. "Logan's little friend? Oh, yes, I believe she was there this afternoon, though I did not quite catch the name."

The producer supplied it. "I suspect you had better memorize it, my dear. Though it seems to have slipped your notice, she is Logan's fiancée. I don't doubt we shall be hearing more of her in the future than we have in the past."

"His fiancée! Of course, I had forgotten," Janine said, the frown that creased her brow serving to convey the impression despite her words, that this was the first she had heard of the matter.

"Have you been enjoying your holiday?" Hobbs asked in polite tones, though the glance he sent from Logan to his wife was sharp.

"Yes indeed. It has done me a world of good; I can't begin to tell you. I know it was silly of me to pack and fly in such a dramatic fashion, but I really had to get away from all the terrible publicity. Why I let it bother me, knowing what all those magazines and newspapers are like, knowing it was all a stupid misunderstanding, I can't say. I suppose I am just too sensitive."

The waiter brought their drinks then, creating a small diversion. As Hobbs ordered for Janine, Clare slanted a quick look at Logan. There was hard anger in his blue eyes. Tactics such as Janine was using were hard to combat, especially in the present circumstances. Watching the way Logan's fingers tightened around his glass, Clare was not certain how long he would even try. If Janine persisted much longer with her coy smiles and insinuations, Clare was afraid he would explode. Was that what the producer's wife wanted? Was she so certain of her husband's affections and her control of the situation that she would risk anything Logan might say, confident that she could twist it to her own advantage? Would Marvin Hobbs believe his wife had been throwing herself at Logan, or would he prefer to believe the accusation was only Logan's way of trying to get out of an entanglement he no longer wanted?

"I don't imagine you have been able to do much skiing?" Marvin Hobbs observed to the table at large.

"No," Logan answered.

"Oh, no," Janine said with a laugh. "You can have no idea of what the weather has been like, or you would not ask such a thing. If it is possible to get cabin fever from being cooped up in a lodge, then that is what I have had. A few hardy souls were on the slopes this morning, but not I. Powder is fine, I love it, but such deep powder is nothing short of an invitation to disaster."

"Do you ski, Clare?"

"I'm afraid not," Clare replied with a polite smile for their host.

"But that's terrible!" Janine exclaimed. "What is the use of coming to Aspen if you don't ski? Something must be done about it. I shall have to take you in hand. That way we will get to know each other better."

"I'm not sure we will be here long enough for that," Logan said.

"No? Such a pity. I could have given Clare quite a few pointers, not only on skiing, of course, but on a number of other things that will come in handy if she is to be one of our little group." The woman paused long enough to give Clare a brittle smile. "Forgive my curiosity, Clare, but I can't help wondering how you came to meet Logan, since you don't ski, and you can't be from L.A. or there would have been some mention of you in the gossip columns."

"We met," Logan said as Clare hesitated, "when Clare requested an interview. She is a writer."

"A writer? How interesting. And who do you work for?"

"I free-lance, personality pieces, mainly," Clare answered.

"I see," Janine murmured, though there was a puzzled look in her narrow green eyes. "I would like to read your article on Logan. Where did it appear, and when?"

"It hasn't," Logan replied with a lazy smile. "I'm afraid we never got around to the interview, what with one thing and another."

"Pity," Janine said, "but I suppose a ring is

better than a story. Do you mind if I see yours, Clare? I'm sure, given Logan's reputation for romanticism and generosity, that it is something spectacular."

"I haven't bought a ring yet," Logan said. "There hasn't been that much time."

"You mean you haven't been engaged long? But I understood you had known each other for some time. I do hope, my dear Logan, that all the furor recently didn't force your hand?"

It was Clare who answered. "I don't know exactly what you mean by that, Mrs. Hobbs," she said, changing positions in her chair so that she leaned a little closer to the actor who was supposed to be her fiancée. "If you must know, Logan wanted to buy me the biggest diamond in Aspen, but I wouldn't hear of it. I didn't want just any ring, but something special. By that, I don't necessarily mean something expensive or bigger and better than anyone else's. I would just prefer to wait for something that is as unique as what we feel for each other."

As if on cue, Logan reached to take in his warm clasp her hand that rested on the table. The touch sent a tingle like an electric shock up her arm.

"How sweet. But if you will take my advice, darling, you won't wait too long. If the engagement were to be called off at this stage, you would have nothing."

Clare, meeting the searching glance of the man beside her with heightened color, said, "If the engagement were called off at this point, I think I would prefer to have no reminders."

Marvin Hobbs grunted and lifted his glass to Clare in a brief salute. "It's too bad more young women don't feel as you do."

Janine Hobbs, busy slipping her fur coat from her shoulders, said nothing. When she looked up again, it was to inquire about her household in Los Angeles. From there, she moved to people and places known only to Logan, her husband, and herself, effectively excluding Clare from the conversation.

They had ordered and their plates had been placed before them when Janine looked up, fixing Logan with a faintly malicious gaze.

"I think you made some mention of business with my husband this afternoon. Am I right in supposing it concerns the screenplay you gave Marvin a copy of to read a month ago?"

"More or less," Logan agreed, "though I am still working on it."

"Oh, really?" Janine turned to her husband. "And are you thinking of taking on the project?"

Marvin Hobbs nodded, his attention on the

prime rib that covered his plate.

"I was afraid of that."

Clare looked up. "Afraid?"

"Yes, and why not? Basically, it's another western, isn't it?" The producer's wife gave a pretty shrug. "No one takes such equine epics seriously."

"It is set in the West, all right," Logan replied in answer to her question, "but the plot bears no resemblance to the type of thing you are talking about, and the theme is important."

"Heaven perserve us from movies with important themes," Janine declared. "The critics may applaud, but the public doesn't want such heavy stuff. It gets in the way of the story. It was Barnum, wasn't it, who said, 'You will never go broke underestimating the public taste'? I'm not advocating a sideshow of freaks, but I've been in this business long enough to know that Shakespeare is not good box office."

"My story may have a historical background, but I doubt anybody could mistake it for Shakespeare," Logan drawled. Beside him, Clare could sense the disgusted rage building within him and the tight leash he held on his temper.

"A costume drama!" Janine sat back with a trill of laughter. "Marvin, did you hear that? You know what poison those have been in the last few years."

As the woman's laugh grated on her nerves, Clare entered the fray. "It seems to me that whether a costume drama is successful or not depends on the production. I don't think you can call *Roots*, which was essentially a costume drama, box-office poison."

"Oh, television!" Janine sneered.

"Whether with television or movies, you are appealing to people who invest their time and attention, as well as their money, in the entertainment you are providing. You can't divide them up into moviegoers and TV viewers. The two groups are interwoven, basically the same people."

"I hadn't realized you were quite such an authority."

"I'm not," Clare said. "Some things only require common sense."

"So long as we know how to value your contribution," Janine said with a superior smile.

A cold light entered Clare's gray eyes. "So far as that goes, perhaps there is another point that needs clarification. Have you read Logan's screenplay, Mrs. Hobbs?"

"No, but I have discussed it with Marvin," Janine said defensively.

"Not the same thing, I think. You can have no idea of the scope and stature of the characters, the color and movement of the tale, its grandeur or its poignancy."

"You speak as though you have read the script."

"Yes, I have, and I think it would be tragic if it is never put on film, not only because of its beauty, but for its contribution to the quality of life for ourselves and our children."

"Well, Janine," Marvin Hobbs said after a long moment of silence, "what do you have to say to that?" When his wife sent him a tight-lipped glare without replying, he turned to Clare. "For myself, I admire your loyalty. It's enough to make a man wonder what there is about the play, or about the man who wrote it, to call forth such a defense. I can see I am going to have to take a long and careful look at this whole thing. That being the case, I have a suggestion. What do you say we all join Janine at this lodge of hers? You, Clare, can learn your way about the slopes while the rest of us get in some exercise. And then after dark we can relax around the fire and discuss this project in detail during those long after-ski evenings."

"I believe," Janine said with a touch of sarcasm, "that the phrase is *après*-ski."

"Thank you," Marvin Hobbs said gravely, then turned back to Clare and Logan. "Well? What do you say?" Clare looked at Logan, waiting for him to decline for her. He avoided her eyes. "Clare and I will have to let you know later, if you don't mind. Say, in the morning?"

The venomous look in Janine Hobbs's green eyes was divided equally among Clare, Logan, and her husband. Marvin Hobbs ignored it. His face bland, inscrutable, he said, "After hearing Clare's plea for your screenplay, I am not certain any longer which one of you will persuade the other to come this time. I can't speak for Janine, but I will be disappointed if you don't join us, both of you."

5

There was no possibility of Clare and Logan discussing Marvin Hobb's proposal until later, much later. The chance did not come, in fact, until Logan saw Clare to the door of her hotel room. Taking the key from her hand, he unlocked the door. Instead of handing it back, he stepped inside the room, waited for her to enter, then closed the door behind them.

Despite the fact that she had slept in the same room with this man for two long nights and spent practically every waking minute in his company, Clare found herself amazingly nervous at being alone with him now. She moved away from him, taking a seat in one of the armchairs on either side of a lamp table at the far end of the room. With her lashes lowered, she toyed with the scalloped lace edge of her sleeves. Logan glanced at the other chair. Rejecting it, he took up a position on the end of the bed across from her.

"Well?" he said, his voice quiet. "Will you do it?"

Clare looked up at him. "Are you serious?"

"I am."

"You actually want me to go on pretending to be your fiancée?"

"So far, I've seen nothing wrong with the way you carry it off."

"Doing it for an evening is one thing," she protested. "Trying to keep it up for several days is something else entirely."

"I will be here to help you. I have had some small experience in making a role believable, you know, and also in supporting other actors."

She gave him a wan smile. "I am not an actress."

"I think you underestimate youself, if this evening is any example. Everything considered, it was good of you to come to my aid and defense. I might even go so far as to say it was inspired."

"You make it sound so calculated. It wasn't like that at all."

"Wasn't it? Whatever the reasons, I am grateful."

"That may be, but it is no reason to jeopardize this deal with Marvin Hobbs," she said earnestly.

"If I didn't believe going on with this farce of an engagement was the best way to bring this deal off, I wouldn't suggest it. I wish Hobbs could judge my script for what it is, without personalities entering into it. That's impossible now; Janine has seen to that. As long as I thought she was sincere in what she was doing, I was willing to overlook it, even to forget the whole thing and find another producer, to keep from coming between her and Marvin. As it is, I have an uncomfortable feeling that it was her vanity and nothing more that was hurt when I refused to play along, and it is spite now that has made her so determined to sabotage the project. Well, I happen to think too much of what I am doing to let her get away with it. I will do whatever is necessary to fight her. Marvin Hobbs likes you. If keeping you with me as my fiancée will encourage him to decide in my favor, then I will do it, if I possibly can."

"Hasn't it occurred to you that I may find it impossible to resist making use of what happens?"

His eyes narrowed. "I will have to trust you, won't I? Maybe it would make you happier if I told you that if you will do as I ask, when this is over I will give you any kind of interview you please."

Clare tilted her head. "Is that a bribe?" she inquired, her tone cool despite the flush across her cheekbones.

"You could call it that."

His offer could be considered in two ways: as a gauge of how much he wanted to see his work produced by Hobbs, and also as a change in his attitude toward both Clare and her writing.

"I'm not certain the damage hasn't already been done. Janine did a pretty thorough job of discrediting the idea this evening."

"You repaired much of the impression she made. I think it's worth a try. I owe the project that much."

Clare nodded and looked away from him. "If I do decide to do it, several things must be understood. Number one, that I have to spend some time with Beverly and her husband. Otherwise, I can make no promises."

"There should be no difficulty about that."

"The second thing is that I will be able to stop at any time it becomes too much for me."

"Agreed."

"And finally, I would like to have an end to sarcastic remarks and accusations. No matter what you may think, I came into this accidentally. Whether I accept your offer of an interview or not, I want it accepted, at least verbally, that I never sought one. If I do as you ask, and if later I write an article, it will be because in both cases I feel that the results will be worth the effort."

He stared at her, an appraising look in his intent blue eyes, as though he were weighing her, coming to some internal conclusion. A current of magnetism seemed to emanate from him, a positive force that made her sit completely still, unable to move, until he released her with an abrupt nod.

Rising with a lithe movement, he held out his hand. "That's fair enough," he said. "It's settled, then. I'll tell Marvin in the morning, and I'll let you know what the plans are after I've talked to him."

"All right," Clare said, her voice husky in her throat.

"It may help you to look on this as a job. Since I asked you to hire on, I'll take care of the expenses."

"That isn't necessary," Clare said firmly. "I prefer to pay my own way. About this hotel room, I want you to have it changed into my name."

"Would you have stayed here, in a place like this, if it hadn't been for dinner this evening?"

"No, of course not —"

"Then I think we can safely say the expense

was due to the project, and should be charged against it."

As Clare looked up at him, she felt her senses assailed once more by the light in his brilliant blue eyes. "I . . . I have the feeling there is something wrong with that logic, but I'm not sure what it is."

"When you decide, let me know. We will have plenty of time to discuss it."

Smiling a little, he dropped a kiss on her forehead, and with quiet, easy footsteps, moved to the door and let himself out of the room.

"Why in the world did you ever agree to such a thing?"

Beverly sat across from Clare in a booth in the hotel coffee shop. Her brown hair hung in a shining pageboy about her heart-shaped face. There was a troubled look in her soft brown eyes, and the happy animation that usually enlivened her features was absent. Leaning forward, she repeated. "Why?"

Clare swirled the steaming coffee around the inside of her cup, then looked up. "I'm not sure. I guess one reason is Janine. I hate to see Logan disappointed because of her petty vindictiveness, and then, she didn't exactly endear herself to me. On top of that is the screenplay.

It really is good, Bev. Something that worth-while deserves a chance."

"Are you trying to tell me it has nothing whatever to do with Logan Longcross? Because if you are, I will have to tell you I find that hard to believe."

"Well, naturally, I am doing it because he asked me. I would never have dreamed of suggesting it myself."

"That is not what I meant, and you know it."

"Do you mean you think I am going along with all this because of some idealistic infatuation with him as a movie star? You are as bad as he is!" Clare's smile took the heat from her words.

"That's what he thinks, does he?"

"It is certainly what he thought at first. I hope I convinced him he was wrong, but it's hard to be sure."

"Oh, yes, instead he thinks you are a lady journalist out to get him. Has it occurred to you, Clare, that he is just using you in much the same way that he thinks you meant to use him to further your career?"

"I can't say it has," Clare answered. "Even if it were true, I can hardly complain, can I?"

"You don't intend to accept his offer of an interview, or mean to write an article, do you?"

"Don't you think I will have earned it?"

"Clare!"

"Oh, yes, I know, I should do my bit, then fade into the background. When no article appears under my by-line, Logan will know he has misjudged me and I will be vindicated. I grant you there would be satisfaction in that, but there might be more in writing something that will let people know what he is really like."

Beverly frowned. "From what you have told me, I'm not sure he would appreciate that."

"Yes," Clare said with a dispirited nod, "you are probably right."

"On the other hand," Beverly went on, "he did offer you the interview. You didn't ask for it as a condition for playing his little game. That must mean something."

"I told you about his reading the tear sheets," Clare said, tapping the sheets of newsprint she had handed over to Beverly. "Maybe it means he approved of my writing."

"I supposed it might," Beverly agreed. She sipped her coffee, then sat back. "If you have made up your mind, there is nothing I can say to stop you. I only hope you know what you are doing."

"I think so. It will only be for a few days."

"You are moving up to the lodge at Snowmass after lunch?"

"Yes, that's right. Bev, I can't tell you how grateful I am to you for not making a fuss. I know I've ruined all your plans for this week."

"Listen," her friend said, an impish smile creeping into her eyes, "don't worry about it. I do want you to come and see the cabin John and I fixed up, but other than that, we will still spend plenty of time together. There are the ski slopes; John and I will be out there helping you learn to ski so you can keep up with the rest of them. Then maybe we can have a few drinks or dinner together one night. It will all be great fun, and," she added, her tone elaborately casual, "if Logan Longcross should be somewhere in your vicinity, I won't complain! I'm not exactly immune to his charm."

"And what, I wonder, would your John say to that?" Clare teased.

"He would say it was fine with him, so long as I didn't get too serious. It's not a bad attitude, now that I think about it. Don't you get too serious either, will you, Clare? I would hate to see you get hurt."

"I wouldn't worry," Clare said, but she was uncomfortably aware that she had not mentioned to Beverly that gentle kiss before Logan had left her room the night before.

126

The morning was sunny and bright, blindingly bright. Clare and Beverly, bundled up to the ears, spent the remainder of it seeing to the business of estimates and insurance forms on her car repairs, and afterward visiting some of the shops in the little Victorian mall. If Clare was going to learn to ski, she would have to have the proper attire. She had debated using waterproofed jeans and sweaters, then decided against it. Janine, she was certain, would be wearing the latest from the ski resorts of Europe. Clare could not hope to compete, of course; still, she did not intend to be entirely outclassed.

She had left the hotel that morning without informing Logan. To begin with, she did not want to give him reason to think she expected his escort everywhere she went. In addition, though she might receive better service following in Logan's wake, she did not particularly care to have her expedition turned into a three-ring circus. There was one other thing. Logan could see to the everyday expenses of the next few days if he pleased, but she did not mean to have him pay for the clothes she wore. There might not be much of the money she had saved for this vacation trip left when she had outfitted herself, but what she wore would be her own. And if she needed justification for such an outlay, she could always tell herself that she would be coming back to visit Beverly; there would be other skiing holidays.

The down-filled parkas, the bib overalls, and the coveralls and matching sweaters seemed to come mainly in vivid primary colors of bright yellow and green, blue and red, or in darker earth tones. It was difficult choosing among them. At last, after much discussion and a trip to the dressing room, Clare decided on an ensemble of warm but lightweight red nylon with sweater-knit cuffs and collar of soft gray and white, and a coordinated sweater and cap of alternating bands of red, gray and white. Beverly, looking at this and that while Clare shopped, had found a matched set of gloves, scarf, and cap that she could not resist. They carried their purchase to the checkout counter.

The woman attendant turned from serving another customer, gave Clare a warm smile that seemed to hold more than a little interest, and began to fold her things, writing down each article on a sales slip, stapled it to the bright-colored plastic bag with its ski motif, and handed it across the counter.

Clare stared at her. "But you haven't told me how much I owe you."

"Why, nothing, my dear. While you were in

the dressing room, the gentleman waiting in the car outside came in and told me I was to send the bill to him at his hotel."

With the package in her arms and a flush on her cheeks, Clare turned, following the direction of the woman's nod. Through the glass door of the shop, a car could be seen, the dark-colored rental car consigned to Logan. A man sat behind the wheel, a man wearing a ski cap and dark glasses. Even if she had not had the advantage of knowing his identity, she thought she would have recognized him anywhere. The shape of his head, the way it sat upon his shoulders, his relaxed, animal grace, were unmistakable.

"Logan?" Beverly asked.

"Logan." Clare's tone was laconic. Turning back to the saleswoman, she said, "I don't care what the gentleman told you, I would rather pay for my own clothes."

"I couldn't let you do that, miss. He expressly told me not to tell you how much it was, or accept payment."

"Is it the policy of this store to refuse cash when it is offered?"

"No, no. But I would hate to disappoint the gentleman, considering who he is, and especially since he asked me so nicely, as a favor to him, to send the bill on."

Another woman under Logan's spell! The sales slip attached to the bag she held had only a list of the items inside; there was no total. Clare drew a deep, calming breath. "Could I see the manager?"

"Certainly. I am the manager," the woman answered, and smiled.

Taking a firmer grip on her package, Clare stepped back to wait while Beverly paid for her knitwear. As soon as she had finished, Clare moved toward the door. She pushed through, with Beverly close behind her, marched to the waiting car, and pulled the door open on the passender side.

Logan turned toward her, a smile curving his mouth. "Through already?"

"What is the idea of having my clothes charged to you?"

"I told you —"

"My skiing clothes were not part of the bargain," Clare interrupted.

"No? I don't very well see how you intend to do without them. The spectacle would be interesting, I will admit, but I have the feeling you would be just a little cold."

She glared at him. "You know what I mean. I intended to go skiing while I was here anyway; I would have had to buy an outfit of some kind."

"Just like the one you have in that bag you are clutching?"

She looked away, unable to sustain his brilliant blue gaze. "I would prefer not to be obligated to you."

"Possibly, but since I am already indebted to you, I prefer to make the situation mutual. Now, are you going to stand there all day, or are you ready to go back to the hotel?"

"Beverly and I," she said distinctly, "have some shopping to do."

"Is this Beverly?" Logan inquired, nodding to Clare's friend, who stood well back, trying not to listen to their conversation, though there was a gleam of repressed amusement in her brown eyes. As Clare made a hurried introduction, Logan sent Beverly one of his heart-stopping smiles by way of acknowledgment.

"You ladies go ahead, then. If you will leave your packages here, I will watch them; then, when you are through, we can have lunch."

Clare, listening to Beverly's quick, almost breathless acceptance of the invitation, watched the exchange with narrowed eyes. It seemed Logan had set himself to please. At this stage it was difficult to tell who his target was. Beverly or herself. If it was the former, then his object might be to discover just how much of Clare's story about her background was true,

131

by questioning her friend over lunch. If he was being so nice for Clare's sake, then she was at a loss to see the reason, unless he was already practicing for his role as fiancée. He must realize, however, that the effort would be wasted on Beverly. Since Beverly knew Clare's movements and schedule so well, it would have been impossible for Clare to keep the truth from her, even if she had wanted to. For that matter, it would also be too much of a strain to keep up the fiction of more shopping, especially in the face of Beverly's rooted reluctance to move on.

When Beverly fell quiet, Clare spoke. "The other things were not important. I can pick them up anytime. We can eat now, if you like."

"I don't mind waiting," Logan said.

"I wouldn't think of it." Clare got into the car and slid across the seat, making room for Beverly. Logan reached for the package she held rather awkwardly in her lap, and turning, placed it on the rear seat. As he settled back, her gray eyes met his in a look of mute suspicion. The audacious grin he gave her did nothing to reassure her.

For luncheon, despite the luxury of their surrounding in the hotel dining room, they chose chili, hot and spicy, with saltine crackers. The hearty fare seemed to go with the snowy view beyond the windows.

Logan, breaking crackers into his bowl, glanced at Beverly. With offhand casualness he said, "I understand your husband is a ski instructor; the GLM method, I suppose?"

"Yes, the graduated-length method of instruction is fairly basic here at Aspen, though the ATM, the American teaching method, is also used, of course, and the basic-turn approach."

"He taught you, I think Clare said?"

"That's how we met."

"I'm sure he is well qualified, but that doesn't mean he is a good teacher. I don't suppose it would help to ask your opinion on that question."

"No," Beverly said on a laugh. "I'm not exactly unbiased. There are those who say he is the best in the area, however. He takes his work seriously. He is an admirer of the techniques of Georges Joubert and the modern French school, especially as they are applied to racing."

"Racing? Does he prefer to work with advanced skiers, then, rather than beginners?"

"No, I don't think so. I know he likes to teach children. He says they are natural skiers. They don't worry about people watching them or what their form looks like; they just do it.

But he really enjoys teaching people to over-come their fears, to relax and take pleasure in what they are doing. According to John, that is the first step in learning to ski really well."

Logan nodded. "It sounds like it will be safe to leave Clare's lessons in his hands, then."

Beverly smiled as if he had just bestowed a great gift upon her. To an inquiry about Clare starting lessons late that afternoon, she gave a quick affirmative, promising to call John as soon as she had finished lunch.

"I will leave you to it, then, this afternoon, while I go back to the house for clothes for a more extended stay," Logan said. "That is, if you have no objections, Clare?"

"None in the world," Clare said.

It was true. She was anxious to get started, and Logan had seen to it that she would do it at least a day earlier than she had thought she might, considering the move from the hotel to the ski lodge this afternoon. Regardless, his highhanded methods annoyed her, and she did not trouble to hide the fact.

Logan, if he noticed, ignored it. Turning back to Beverly, he asked. "Have you known Clare long?"

"Forever," Beverly answered. "We went to high school and secretarial college together, had our first job together at desks not six feet apart."

"What kind of job was that?"

Beverly answered, and the questions went on. They seemed idle, interspersed with rambling stories of his own boyhood, and yet their purpose could not have been more clear. Clare had been right. Logan had set out to gain information, and that was exactly what he was getting. From the glances she threw at her now and then, Clare thought her friend realized it well enough, but she seemed at a loss as to how to put a stop to the pleasant inquisition.

Clare was not. Quietly seething, she put down her spoon, touched her napkin to her lips, and placed it on the table.

"Are you satisfied now?" she asked, her voice quiet but the gray of her eyes dark as they rested upon Logan.

"Not quite," he said lightly. "I thought hot apple strudel for dessert. How does that sound to you? I recommend it. It's good here, and you are going to need all the energy you can get this afternoon."

He sat watching her with one brow lifted, waiting to see if she meant to challenge his deliberate misunderstanding of her question, or if she would accept the compromise he offered and call a truce. She would accept, but on her own terms.

"The strudel sounds delicious. As you say, I expect I will need energy. I don't doubt I will also need that roaring fire and hot spiced wine we nonskiers are always hearing about, later on this evening. And I am sure that if they have to put up with my clumsiness for long this afternoon, Beverly and John will be glad of a little refreshment. I hope you don't mind if I bring them back with me to the lodge this evening when the lesson is over?"

"A great idea. I was just going to suggest it myself, only I hope they will stay for dinner as well."

Beverly looked from one to the other. "I'm sure John would love to," she said, "if it isn't going to be too formal. My John is a lovely man, but he was something of a hippie in his mad youth, and though he will dress for dinner, he is never too thrilled with the idea."

"Informal it will be. That's settled, then," Logan said.

"Yes, it's settled," Clare agreed, and did not look away as she met his mocking blue gaze.

6

The ski area to which Aspen gave its name included an awesome collection of slopes and trails ranging over four different mountains. Each mountain had its own resort community. There was Aspen Mountains, Aspen Highlands, Buttermilk, and finally, Snowmass. The last of the four resorts to be built, Snowmass was also the most exclusive. It was not for the beginning skier, the timid, or those on a budget. It was famed for its size, covering 1,400 acres, for its vertical drop of 3,500 feet, and for its extended deep powder runs, the longest being three and a half miles. It was here that the lodge Janine Hobbs had chosen was located.

Though Beverly had described the resort where her husband sometimes gave private lessons to famous people, Clare was not prepared for the sheer size and scope of it. Built at the foot of Snowmass Mountain, it climbed the slope in neat terraces that followed the winding, well-kept roads. Composed primarily of condominiums, town-house apartments, and ski lodges designed with natural-wood exteriors, cedar shingles, and wide expanses of glass, it exuded an air of planned peace and seclusion. With the ski lifts running and bright ski clothing and equipment everywhere, there was also a sense of subdued excitement. Above the snow-covered roofs towered Snowmass Mountain, over fourteen thousand feet high, with the snaking trails of its ski runs descending all the way from near its summit to what appeared to be the back door of the lodges, each run distinct as it cut a swath through evergreens, and gray, bare-branched aspens.

Driving along the curving entrance road with the snow piled on its shoulders by the plows, Clare could see skiers on the slopes, made tiny by the distance, as they flashed down the mountainside with incredible speed and dexterity. That she would ever be able to do that seemed to Clare improbable, if not impossible.

The style of the lodge, like the other buildings of the resort, was eclectic, a blend of modern natural and rustic designs. It was built in a large square with an attached portico reminiscent of a Bavarian hunting lodge. Inside, it opened into a large area centered with a heated swimming pool edged with green plants, covered overhead by a reinforced Plexiglas dome. The water steamed gently in the bright daylight from above, almost obscuring the tables and chairs set in a small open area at the far end. The rooms rose in tiers around the pool, each of the several floors with its protecting balustrade, so that guests, as they made their way to and from their rooms along the carpeted balconies, could look down into the pool or across the open space to the doors lining the walls of the enclosing sides.

Marvin Hobbs, in what Clare was coming to recognize as his usual highhanded manner, had called to make reservations for the rooms. Janine was accommodated on the floor of rooms just above the pool, since she had been making vigorous use of it, and her husband had managed to secure the suite next door. Clare and Logan found themselves in adjoining rooms two floors higher on the opposite side of the pool.

Logan, entering Clare's room with her to be certain she would be comfortable, noticed the look on her face as she flicked a glance at the convenient connecting door between his room and her own. He tipped the bellhop and closed the door behind him.

"I can have the room changed, if you like," he offered, turning to Clare, a smile lurking at the back of his eyes, though his tone was courteous.

Clare hesitated a moment, then shook her head. "If you are not worried that I will make a nuisance of myself, there is no reason for a change."

He stared down at her. "Am I supposed to be flattered at your confidence in me?"

"Not really, not so long as there is a nice stout lock on this side of the door."

"I see," he answered.

The strong brooding sound he injected into his voice made her look up. "Of course, if your ego is wounded, I can make a point of banging on your door now and then. You could then have the satisfaction of refusing to let me in."

Turning, he strode to the outside door and pulled it open. "Never mind," he said, "I might be tempted to do just the opposite." Stepping out onto the interior balcony, he closed the door quietly behind him.

By the time Clare had donned her ski togs, Beverly had retrieved her four-wheel-drive jeep from in front of the dress shop, where she had left it during lunch, and followed after them. John would have a couple of hours before dark to teach Clare the basics, but in the meantime, Clare was to rent her equipment and get out onto the snow. The best slopes for beginners at Snowmass, according to Beverly's most often quoted authority, her John, were at the golf course of the Snowmass Country Club. The gentle ups and downs and frequent flat stretches of the course were ideal for the first straight runs at walking speed that would help her find her balance.

John found them on the golf course. A sandy-haired, bearded young man of medium height, he had a keen look in his brown eyes as he took note of Clare's size and shape, the length of her skis, and the type of boots and bindings she had been given. When introductions were done, he gave Clare a nod and a friendly smile.

"You seem to be in good shape," he said.

"He means as far as health and equipment are concerned," Beverly explained as Clare blinked and glanced down at her stance upon her skis.

"She thinks that's what I mean," John said with a droll smile and a tilt of his head in the direction of his wife, who was scowling in mock jealousy.

And then the lessons began in earnest. Clare learned how to stand, relaxed with the knees slightly flexed and the soles of her feet pressed firmly against the inner soles of her boots from toes to heels. She discovered how to feel the snow beneath her sliding skis, and how to assume a low position at the end of a run to stop herself. The slopes she was allowed to schuss – ski down in a straight, swift run – grew higher and longer. She advanced to a stepped turn, to a gliding snowplow as a means of slowing or stopping, leading up to the sliding, twisting natural stop she had seen so often employed by professional skiers on television. Her confidence and sense of exhilaration increased as she learned. The cold, thin mountain air, the possibility of onlookers, did not trouble her. Nothing mattered but the glinting white powder beneath her fast-traveling skis. It was with something like shock that she looked up and saw the light fading from the sky and the pink afterglow of the twilight casting lavender shadows across the snow fields.

A blazing fire and something hot to drink were waiting for them all when they returned to the lodge. Only as Clare entered the warm building did she realize how icy the air outside had become. The leaping flames, the dimness of the lounge, the rich smell of coffee and hot chocolate, and the sharp spice scent of mulled wine were exactly what she needed.

Logan, already ensconced at a large round table near the fire with Janine and Marvin Hobbs, held a chair for Clare. When she was seated, he made Beverly and John known to the other couple. No sooner was everyone settled than Janine began to complain about the heat of the fire. John, sitting on her right halfway around the table, at the farthest remove from the great moss-rock hearth, offered to change places with her, but with a pettish shrug she declined. Clare glanced at Logan, her lips pressed tightly together to keep from smiling. An exchange with John would have placed Janine between Beverly and Janine's husband, not the position the producer's wife had had in mind at all.

Whether deliberately or as a simple coincidence, Hobbs turned his back on his wife and began to question John about his work, the profits to be made from a ski resort, and the return to its investors.

Under the cover of their conversation, Logan turned to Clare. "How did it go today?" he asked quietly.

"Fine, as far as I'm concerned," she answered, "though I don't know what John would say."

Beverly, her attention caught by the question, leaned to answer. "He would say you were great. You have a natural talent for skiing, and excellent balance. He told me while we were taking off our coats upstairs that he wouldn't be surprised if you were parallel-skiing in a couple of days, and on the intermediate slopes by the end of the week."

"If I do, it will be because I had a great teacher."

"That's fine, but how do you feel?" Logan queried.

Clare laughed. "Tired, and a little stiff."

"Just wait until in the morning. Ouch!" Beverly whispered.

"Your cheeks are sun- and windburned," Logan said, reaching out to touch the skin of Clare's face with the back of one knuckle. "Right now it's just enough to make you look bright-eyed and healthy, but you have to watch it at this altitude, so close to the sun. Tomorrow you will need a moisturizer and sunscreen."

"Yes and a lip balm of some sort," Clare agreed ruefully.

Logan's gaze rested on the glowing pink curves of her mouth for a long moment. "Yes," he said at last, and picked up his coffeecup.

They progressed from thawing out in the firelit lounge to dinner in the main dining room. Due to her vigorous exercise, Clare's appetite knew no bounds. Not even Janine's shudder and stare as she announced the fact could diminish it a whit. Logan took it in stride. With his hand on one side of her menu, he leaned close to offer his suggestions and amused encouragement. Her order, when at last he gave it to the waiter, matched his dish for dish, a bit of togetherness that caused Beverly to send Clare a sparkling look. An instant later, catching Janine's sharp glance on her, Beverly began to bemoan the fact that Clare could eat anything she wanted and never show a sign, while she herself gained weight from the mere smell of food.

With lips compressed, Janine turned John and began to question him on the various places he had taught skiing. The discovery that he had spent a winter season in the French Alps was enough to galvanize her interest. She smiled upon him with the air of one cosmopolitan meeting another among a crowd of provincials, and showered him with eager queries. Only as the conversation veered away from the difference between French and American techniques, ski lifts, and slope upkeep to the towns, did her enthusiasm lag. This was caused mainly by John's firm refusal to recognize any of the more exclusive shops and hotels she mentioned.

While she listened, Clare played idly with her water glass, turning it in her fingers. Logan shifted in his chair, then reached out to take her hand, chilled by the ice-filled glass, in his warm grasp. As Clare turned, startled, he smiled, his grip tightening a fraction. Clare relaxed by degrees, letting her fingers lie still, trying to assume a fond expression as she met his eyes.

It was not a good effort, she was afraid. It was difficult to appear calm and loving when her nerves were on edge and she was much too aware of the man beside her. Tonight he wore a cable-knit sweater in a beige-and-blue pattern with a pair of well-worn jeans. Despite the casual dress, he was so vital he looked anything but casual. Clare felt the force of his attraction, against her will. It seemed quite possible that if she were the impressionable type, if she were less on her guard, the attention Logan Longcross was paying her might well turn her head.

Dinner was followed by dancing on a floor of translucent Plexiglas to one side of the dining room. Much of the music was fast, with a disco beat accompanied by the pulsing of colored lights under the floor. The noise quickly put an end to conversation. Soon a blue haze of cigarette smoke hung over the tables. The room became overheated and airless.

"Would you like to dance?" Logan leaned close to ask the question, since it was the only way he could be heard. The music was a slow instrumental for a change, but the amplification no less loud.

Clare got to her feet by way of an answer, and made her way through the tables to the floor. Turning, she smiled as she went into Logan's arms. They moved together with precision in a perfect adjustment of height and frame. At first Clare felt awkward, and then, as she realized that Logan knew what he was doing, that he had the easy rhythm that made dancing a natural physical exercise, not a mental discipline, she relaxed. Together they moved to the music, caught in its gentle, reflective mood. Once Clare drew back to look up at Logan. His eyes held hers for long moments. The lights thrown upward from beneath them cast strange wavering shadows over his features, giving them an intimate, almost tender cast of expression that should not have been there. Clare was certain it was a trick of the light, for as they shifted positions, that look disappeared.

The music came to an end. John and Beverly, exchanging one of those glances of unspoken communication between married couples, got to their feet as Clare and Logan returned to the table.

"We hate to break up the party, but I expect we had better be heading home. John has to get up early for work in the morning."

Knowing it was true, Clare did not protest, only contenting herself with expressing her appreciation for the skiing lessons and her enjoyment of the evening. She and Beverly made plans for her to drive out to see the cabin the following morning, and the couple took their leave.

"Nice people," Hobbs commented when they were out of hearing.

Janine, carefully flicking the ash from her cigarette into the tray in the center of the table, said nothing.

"Yes, they are," Logan answered.

There was extra warmth in Clare's gray eyes as she glanced at the man beside her. Noticing he was holding her chair, she shook her head. "I think I will go up to my room. After all that exercise this evening, I am sleepy beyond belief, and it's so stuffy in here I seem to be getting a headache."

"I'll come with you," Logan said.

"There's no need —"

Logan's firm grip on her elbow brought her words to a stumbling halt. "But I want to," he said, his tone caressing.

Marvin Hobbs smiled. "I'll just say good night, then, and hope to see you in the morning. Right now, I think I'll stay where I am and have another drink. What do you say, Janine?"

Clare and Logan did not wait for her answer, but made their brief good nights, and turned toward the exit.

The pool area was dim, lit only by the underwater lights and the clear moonlight coming through the dome overhead. Clare paused in the darkness under the balcony outside the dining room and breathed deep of the cooler air in this high, open space.

"Do you really have a headache?" Logan asked, his voice quiet.

Clare nodded. It was still there, despite the fading sound of the music, reduced to a low, throbbing base from the room a short distance behind them. "Yes, and why not? You must admit this masquerade is something of a strain, or doesn't it affect you that way?"

"No, I don't think it does."

She slanted him a quick glance, unreasonably annoyed by his positive tone. "But then, you are used to playing roles, aren't you, and I'm not."

Logan turned to give her his attention. His

gaze traveled beyond her to the darkness behind them; then, with a swift step he pulled her into his arms, smothering her last words against her lips. His mouth burned on hers. His hold was steely. His kiss deepened as he drew her closer against his chest. Clare's senses reeled, and her lips felt on fire. Her hands, pressed to the broad hardness of his chest, lost their strength. She seemed to feel the millrace of the blood in her veins, and at the same time the driving beat of his heart.

"Excuse me!"

The words, cold, distant, feminine, came from behind Clare. The voice belonged to Janine Hobbs.

His movements unhurried, Logan lifted his head. Smoothing the palms of his hands along Clare's arms without so much as a glance in the other woman's direction, he asked, "Are we blocking your way, Janine?"

"No," she said shortly. "I only followed you to ask if you mean to go out onto the slopes in the morning or if you are visiting Clare's friends with her."

"I expect I will strap on a pair of skis," he answered, without taking his gaze from Clare, his voice so abstracted and uncaring as to be almost insulting.

"You surprise me. I wasn't sure the two of

150

you could bear to be separated that long."

"It will be hard, but we will have the thought of our reunion to sustain us," Logan said dryly, "won't we, darling?"

For an answer, Clare allowed an impish smile to tilt the corners of her mouth. With considerable daring she slid her hands upward until they met behind his neck. Immediately he drew her close once more, locking his fingers behind her waist.

Janine made a sound that might have indicated anger or disgust. Hard upon it she pushed past them and continued around the pool to the faintly lighted elevator alcove.

Clare watched her with troubled eyes. "Do you think she heard us?" she asked finally.

"Who can tell?" Logan said, his tone even. "I expect if she did, we will find out, just as soon as she decides what to do about it."

As if suddenly noticing that he still held her, he released his grip and stepped back. He stared down at Clare's pale face in the dim light, his own features masklike and unreadable.

Across the width of the pool the elevator doors slid open and Janine stepped inside the lighted car. The doors hissed shut, and there came a familiar hum as it rode upward.

"Shall we go?" Logan said, and with a touch led her out of the dimness toward the empty alcove.

7

Beverly's cabin, for all its small size, had the comfortable feeling of a home. Macrame wall hangings and crewelwork pictures softened the severity of paneled walls. There were Indian rugs on the polished wood floors, mixed with braided and hooked rugs in neutral colors. Dried flowers and lengths of weathered wood in interesting shapes ornamented the mantel of the smoke-blackened stone fireplace, and in one window was a collection of woven baskets and trays showing the black and sand colors of Indian designs.

The mint-and-lemon smell of herb tea, one of Beverly's more recent enthusiasms, filled the room. Beverly, sitting across from Clare at an antique pedestal dining table, set down her stoneware mug and stared at her friend.

"I would not be in your shoes, Clare," she

said slowly, "for anything in the world. To have to put up with that Hobbs woman, with her saccharine sweetness and her sharp little digs when you are not looking, would drive me wild. Last night I wasn't even involved, and was ready to pull her hair out. And then this nerve-racking business of playing up to Logan while he makes love to you, forcing yourself all the time to remain unmoved; maddening! I'm not sure it wouldn't be best, all things considered, if Janine Hobbs didn't tumble to Logan's little game."

"You may be right," Clare admitted. "It's just that this screenplay means so much to him."

"Are you sure it's not that you would hate to see the game come to an end?"

"Oh, Bev, of course not!"

"Not that I would blame you. He can be devastating when he sets his mind to it. That's just it. He has set his mind to it."

Clare looked down into the pale green liquid in her cup. "You make him sound so self-centered."

"Isn't he?"

"I don't think so. At least, I know he would prefer not to be. He was forced into it this time, as much by the strength of his beliefs as Janine's interference. Besides, I'm not certain everything he does is for his own purposes. He respects Marvin Hobbs for his talent as a producer and his contributions to the film industry, and I believe he genuinely likes you and John."

"I will admit he was easier to talk to than I expected," Beverly said. "In fact, other than his preoccupation with his privacy, he hardly seems like a superstar at all. I mean, where is his entourage? I thought people like him traveled with bodyguards, secretaries, and masseurs, to say nothing of beautiful unattached women. Where are his women?"

Clare laughed. "For the moment, you are looking at her. No, Bev, you are a victim of the propaganda put out by the fan magazines and supermarket papers. If all actors who made it big lived on that scale, they wouldn't have anything left to invest against the time when a fickle public finds a new hero. But enough about Logan and me and my concerns. I liked your John. If he was ever a hippie, he seems to have mellowed. I would say he is satisfied with his life as a married man and the job he is doing."

"Yes, I think so," Beverly agreed.

"I really like what you have done with this cabin. You are lucky to have it, and your John. All you need now is a family."

"That will come eventually." Beverly said; then her smile turned to a look of concern. "You miss that, don't you, Clare, having a home and family? It's important, I know, but you still have your talent as a writer, and a career of some kind, whether it is in real estate or with a newspaper."

"You are right," Clare said. "The only trouble is, I'm greedy. I want it all."

Beverly gave her an obliging smile, and they moved on to other things, though Clare, looking around her from time to time, knew her friend was right. She did miss having a home and someone to care for, missed that sense of belonging, missed having someone to share triumphs and disappointments and fears, and the comedy of small everyday events. The latter was one of the few things that she had found enjoyable about the past few days with Logan. More than once their glances had caught in a silent appreciation of the comical aspects of their situation.

It was as Clare was leaving that Beverly, a reluctant and troubled look on her face, asked a final question.

"Clare? Has it occurred to you that Logan might actually be attracted to you?"

"Bev! How can you suggest such a thing after all the warning against it?"

"I don't know. It's just that if he isn't, he is an extremely good actor."

"That's exactly what he is," Clare replied, smiling wryly to cover the sudden ache in the region of her heart.

It was midafternoon when Clare arrived back at the lodge. The place was quiet, nearly deserted except for a lone swimmer, a woman in a black satin-jersey maillot with her short hair lying like pointed petals on her forehead as she swam with slow grace up and down the length of the pool. The other guests were on the slopes, no doubt, taking advantage of the fine weather.

Clare, skirting the pool on her way to the elevator, smiled and spoke a word of greeting as Janine lifted her hand in a brief wave. She thought Janine made a gesture, inviting her to join her in the water, but she pretended she did not see. After the night before, she was not anxious for a tête-à-tête with the other woman.

At the fourth-floor landing, while she hunted for her room key in her bag, she glanced over the balcony railing, Janine had left the pool. Standing slim and straight beside it, she patted herself dry with a scarlet bath sheet, then reached to pick up a black jersey wrap splashed with scarlet flowers. With quick movements she shrugged into it and tied the belt tightly at the waist. Stepping into a pair of sandals, she shook back her hair and turned toward the elevator. Clare, with the tightness of nerves in her chest, turned away, letting herself into her room.

She put down her tote bag and began to take off her coat. She was just putting it away in the closet when a knock came on the door. Clare went still; then, squaring her shoulders, she moved to answer it.

"Hello, Clare," Janine said. "May I come in? I would like to talk to you."

Clare stepped back, then indicated a chair with a wave of her hand as she closed the door. In an effort to postpone the inevitable moment, she said, "I didn't expect to see you inside on a day like this."

"I stayed out several hours this morning. I let Marvin and Logan go without me after lunch because I have an appointment to have my hair done, and because I wanted a few words with you."

"Oh?" The woman was not going to be distracted. Assuming an expression she hoped contained no more than polite interest, Clare sat down on the end of the bed and prepared to listen.

Janine Hobbs leaned back, a cool smile on her red lips as she surveyed Clare. "I heard you and Logan last night, you know. A most interesting and enlightening conversation."

"Last night?" Clare asked, knitting her brows in a troubled frown. "I don't think I understand?"

"I believe you do. You spoke of a masquerade, of playing a role. I think, my dear Clare, that you are no more Logan's fiancée than I am."

A cold feeling moved over Clare. For a fierce instant she wished Logan was there. He would know how to handle this situation. But then, so did she. If she was not going to admit to this woman that she was right, she must convince her that she was wrong.

Summoning a laugh, Clare said, "You must be joking."

"I assure you I am not. Up until last night, I was at a loss to explain you. Oh, I know Logan said there was someone else, but I had the feeling that he was clutching at straws, trying to find some pretext to keep from becoming too seriously involved with me. Logan has a strong sense of honor; it's amazing, really, after all his years on the Coast. He never put it into so many words, but I believe he was actually reluctant to break up my marriage, to take the wife of a man who had been such a close associate, his producer. The pain of telling me so blatant a lie about there being another woman, of forcing himself to give me up, was what brought him here to the mountains. He should have known I would follow him."

"I haven't the most remote idea what you are talking about," Clare said, distaste for the woman's twisted version of the story Logan had told her making her voice hard.

"The evidence is overwhelming against you, Clare. I don't know why I was taken in for a moment, except that I was hurt that Logan could leave me like that, with such an appearance of carelessness. I didn't know to what desperate lengths he was willing to go to protect himself from his feelings for me."

"I dislike to cause you any more pain and embarrassment." Clare said, "but I think it would be best if you could bring yourself to accept the truth of my engagement to Logan."

"Without a shred of proof? What kind of a fool do you think I am? No, I will tell you why you are lying. First of all, you have no ring. Logan would never have left such an important detail until some vague future date."

"I told you the reason for that. The proposal was not something he planned; it just happened. You could hardly expect him to go dashing out into a blizzard for such a thing. I would not have let him."

As if she had not heard, Janine went on. "No one has ever heard of you, ever seen you with Logan before."

"Logan's preference for privacy, even secrecy, concerning his private life is well-known."

"You appeared in your role only after Marvin had surprised you alone with Logan at his retreat."

"Are you suggesting Logan claimed me as his fiancée merely to save my reputation? Don't be ridiculous. Besides, the notion is so old-fashioned as to be laughable."

"I don't think you would have cared at all. It would probably have been quite a feather in your cap, even if news of your presence in such a love nest had been splashed over every news-stand in the country. No, I don't think your reputation was involved. Logan may be conventional, but he isn't stupid. Nor do I think he would have done it to improve Marvin's opinion of him. Marvin has some outdated ideas of his own about fidelity and morality, but he is a realist, especially when it comes to people involved with the movie business."

"I suppose you do have some kind of a theory?" Clare inquired with a show of weariness.

"Yes, I do. It was for my sake, to protect me,

of course. You were there. Marvin already thought you were Logan's — shall we say special friend? — for the week. Logan decided to use the situation to convince Marvin he had absolutely no grounds for his suspicions of me."

Janine's incredible self-confidence was beginning to wear on Clare. Wasn't it just possible her version of the story was the correct one? Logan had used violence to protect the producer's wife once; why wouldn't he do this for her also? The reasons for the slight changes he had made in the story could be easily explained. He might have thought Clare would be more sympathetic, more easily persuaded to do as he wanted, if she thought he was unattached. The gentleman actor being pursued by a woman he did not want to hurt and could not afford to anger. At the same time, the tale would have served to mask his true feelings. It was plausible, and yet Clare was not ready to accept it completely.

In her best imitation of Logan's mocking style, Clare said, "It was lucky that I happened to be around when I was needed, then, wasn't it?"

"That did confuse me at first," Janine admitted. "I had the best of reasons for knowing Logan had no interest in the company

162

of other women. Forgetting in another woman's arms is not his style; he is stronger than that. How did you come to be there, then? I asked myself, and I remembered the small clue Logan had supplied. You are a free-lance writer. The instant I remembered, I knew. You were there for a story."

"Logan doesn't give out interviews," Clare pointed out.

"You are not from the Coast, not too familiar with interviewing big stars, I think. You wouldn't know Logan's habits until it was too late. I don't know how you came to discover where he was, but I expect the blizzard caught you at Logan's place. You must be thanking your lucky stars for it. Not only did it give you time enough with him to come up with some kind of story, regardless of his lack of cooperation, it landed you a temporary post as his fiancée — not to mention a chance to be closer to him than most women ever dreamed. Was that last prospect all it took to induce you to agree to this — what did you call it? — masquerade, or did he offer you something else? Say, an exclusive?"

"You have it all worked out, don't you?" Clare asked. "I don't see why you didn't want to speak of it in front of Logan, then. Could it be because you are afraid he will deny it?"

She was troubled by more than that. Janine had come so close to the truth Clare felt a sickness in the pit of her stomach. It was odd, but the closer she came, the less inclined Clare felt to admit to Janine she was right. The fact that both Janine and Logan had hit upon the same reason for her presence at Logan's place was distressing. It might stem from no more than their cynical disbelief in coincidence, bred in the movie capital, but it could also mean that Janine had spoken to Logan already, that he had told her exactly what had taken place between Clare and himself.

"My reasons for not speaking to Logan are no concern of yours," Janine informed her. "Nor is my relationship with him any of your business. It must be obvious that we have been, are now, more than friends."

"That isn't the way I heard it," Clare said stubbornly.

"No? You would be a fool to believe any tale Logan might have spun for you to enlist your aid. I tell you what I say is true. Since that is clear, I believe we can dispense with the supposition and the pretense." Janine got to her feet, moving toward the door.

Clare rose also. "Really, I don't know what you are talking about."

"My purpose in coming here this afternoon,"

the former actress went on, her trained voice overriding Clare's with little effort, "was to let you know that I am in possession of the facts. I will condone your part in it because of the stupid screenplay Logan is so determined to have Marvin produce. I care that much for him. My patience is not infinite, however. I have no liking for seeing you pushing yourself into Logan's arms. If you cannot remember that you are a substitute for me, that this masquerade is not reality, then I refuse to be responsible for what I might do. You see, I care more for the man than for his script, and I am growing tired of having to pacify my husband. If you can't be sensible, if you can't be circumspect in your behavior, I will go to Marvin and tell him everything. You keep that in mind the next time Logan makes love to you in public!"

The door slammed behind the woman. Clare stood still, paralzed with anger and fear and a deeper dread that she approached cautiously in her mind. Could Janine be right? Was it really possible? Had Logan lied to her? Beyond this question was one other haunting doubt, one other possibility. Logan could have lied to them both. It would have been to his advantage, if he had been somewhat less than particular as to ethics, for him to play up Janine in order to win her influence with her husband; then, when she became too intense, threatening to leave her husband regardless of the loss to Logan of Hobbs' support, he might have decided to skip town, hoping she would do nothing so long as he was not there to support her. When Marvin Hobbs had confronted Logan, obviously expecting to find his wife, Logan had grasped at Clare to protect himself, later offering her a plausible tale and a likely bribe to gain her cooperation. Meanwhile, he had persuaded Janine to remain docile, at least until the contracts for the film had been signed.

The explanation made sense. It did not fit her conception of Logan's character, but he was an actor, wasn't he? He could be convincing in any role he chose to play.

For long moments Clare stood in the center of the room, her gray eyes wide and dark with pain, her arms clasped across her body. Though the room was warm, so warm the windows were fogged over, she was suddenly cold, shaken by a chill that came from the drafty emptiness within her.

8

In spite of the fullness of the next few days, they seemed to creep past. They began early. Clare and Logan breakfasted alone most of the time. Afterward they would drive out into the countryside, sometimes to where the Roaring Fork River lay frozen in its bed, trickling quietly, as if murmuring to itself, beneath the thick layers of greenish-white ice. Other times they would turn east on the narrow, winding road that led to Independence Pass over the Continental Divide, enjoying the majestic snow-covered vistas for as far as the road would take them. Once started, Clare always wanted to go higher and higher, but the mountain pass with its steep grade and unguarded curves was closed for the winter. Once they parked their car at the farthest point the road would take them, and on rented snowshoes, carrying a knapsack loaded with snacks and a flask of hot coffee, tracked through the silent white forests. Once their mode of transporation was cross-country skis, and Clare, sliding along with energy in Logan's wake, was not certain she did not prefer this almost solitary sport to the crowds and competitive daring of the ski slopes.

The slopes were not ignored, however. Clare and Logan drove out once or twice to the resorts at Aspen and Aspen Highlands, where Logan gave Clare pointers on style as they watched the skiers make their runs. One day, following the crowd to Buttermilk, they caught a portion of the national skiing championships, a fine display of technique in the cold winter sunshine.

Clare's own ability on skis improved with each day's lesson. By the time her first week in the mountains was drawing to a close, she had progressed from the grounds of the Snowmass Country Club to the beginner's slope, and from there to intermediate skiing.

Though the daylight hours were spent with Logan almost constantly at her side, the evenings were the worst. When they were alone, or even in the company of Beverly and John, they could meet in cool friendliness, like travelers thrown together for a space of days who would never meet again. All that changed when the sun set behind the mountains. Janine Hobbs insisted on their meeting with her husband and herself for the daily *après*-ski ritual, and afterward for dinner. It was then that Logan became more possessive, more the lover. The change was a subtle one, expressed in a touch, a gesture, a warm glance from which Clare, try as she might, could not look away. With the same effortless ease with which he projected emotion on the screen, he created between them an air of such intimate tenderness that Clare sometimes had to bring herself up short, reminding herself that it had no more substance than celluloid romance.

Still, if she was ever in danger of forgetting, there was always Janine. The woman watched constantly, her eyes slitted and a tight smile on her face. As the nights went by one by one, the producer's wife grew more snappish. She found fault with the drinks served to her, declared that the smell of the woodsmoke nauseated her, and pronounced the band in the dining room as amateurish, certainly not up to the quality of the bands found in the nightspots in Los Angeles. Nothing, not her husband's sarcastic rejoinders or Logan's quiet teasing, could persuade her to leave off her ill humor. If either of the two men guessed the cause of it, they gave no sign. To Clare it was plain enough. The producer's wife resented even a pretense of interest in Clare from Logan. Not that there had ever been any doubt. It had been Janine's jealousy that had driven the woman to threaten putting an end to the bogus engagement. Sometimes Clare, sitting self-consciously in the circle of Logan's arms, watched by that basilisk stare, was not at all sure it would be a bad thing if she did.

On this particular evening, they had dined on Alaskan king crab, a truly delicious change from beef, one that Clare, coming from a state famous for seafood, had never tried. The band had been replaced for the night by a guitarist, an excellent performer who played in the classic Spanish style through the meal, turning later to folk songs and popular country-and-western tunes, encouraging everyone to sing along. The idea found favor with all except Janine. Too utterly junior college, she sneered, and sat tight-lipped as the others raised their voices around her.

To Clare, it was great fun. Her voice was clear and strong, and she enjoyed singing. Moreover, the shared music was much closer to what she had expected of entertainment at a ski lodge than the cacophony of hard rock. Logan joined in also, though with less enthusiasm. He seemed more preoccupied with watching Clare's enjoyment, the sparkle in her eyes and her pleasure in the recognition of favorite melodies and lyrics. Once he leaned close to harmonize, and when she turned to him with a grin when the song was over, gave her a brief hug, pressing a light kiss to the corner of her mouth.

Clare stiffened, drawing away. She slanted a quick look at Janine. The woman was stabbing out her cigarette in the ashtray, crushing it as she stared at Logan with hooded eyelids heavy with mascara.

Logan touched Clare's arm. "What is it, darling?" he asked, his voice low.

The endearment, the soft concerned tone, did not escape Janine. The color drained from her face, leaving it white with anger.

Clare shook her head. "Nothing," she murmured. As Logan drew her back against him once more, her gaze flicked to Marvin Hobbs. With a frown between his eyes and his mouth in a thin line, he was watching his wife. Slowly he turned toward Logan. It was Clare who intercepted his hard stare, however. Immediately his face smoothed to blandness, though there was a perceptible glint in the depths of his eyes.

The evening wore on. Marvin left the table

to speak to an acquaintance he had made during the course of the last days. After a few minutes he waved to catch Logan's attention and motioned to him. As soon as Logan was out of hearing, Janine leaned toward Clare.

"What do you think you are doing?" she hissed. "Flirting, practically begging to be fondled and petted before my very eyes. I warned you what would happen if you pushed me too far!"

"If you aren't careful, your husband is going to catch on, whether you are ready to tell him or not," Clare answered as easily as she could manage.

"What do you mean?"

"He was watching you turn green with envy just now."

"Is that so? Little I care! He won't do a thing about it."

"I wouldn't be too sure, if I were you. I don't think I would care to cross him."

Janine shrugged. "You have to know how to handle him, but it was not my husband we were discussing, it was you."

"Yes, you don't like the way I am behaving. If you remember, I didn't kiss Logan, he kissed me. According to you, there is nothing to it, so I fail to see why you are upset. If you have some complaint to make on that score, I suggest you make it to him. I am sure if you are what you say you are to each other, the last thing Logan will want is to annoy you."

Janine threw herself back in her chair so hard it creaked. "I never have a chance to see him alone. He is with you most of the day, and Marvin dogs my footsteps every evening."

"I expect if what you told me the other day is true, not meeting is the wisest course."

"Wise?" Janine laughed, a hollow sound. "What do I care about being wise? That would be a poor kind of love."

"I was under the impression the wisdom was on Logan's part," Clare said, her smile innocent.

The other woman sent her a sharp look. "I will find a way," she muttered, and turned to smile at Logan as he threaded his way back to their table.

At last the dreadful evening was done. The time came when Clare could retire to her room and close the door behind her. She washed her face to remove her makeup and donned her nightgown, a long sheath of apricot silk with a mandarin collar and side seams slit to well above the knees. In an effort to relax she brushed her hair, spreading the silken blond strands upon her shoulders like a cape. Fine tendrils curled about her face, framing her wide, dark eyes, giving her a look of gentle vulnerability. With a sudden movement, Clare put down the brush and swung from the mirror.

She could not sleep. She tossed and turned for what seemed like hours, but when she turned on the bedside lamp and picked up her wristwatch, it had been only an hour and a half. In the bottom of her suitcase was a paperback book. She got it out and sat turning the pages, only to realize after a time that she had read line after line without being able to absorb their meaning. She could not concentrate, could not keep her mind on the story. Her thoughts went around in endless circles. Why had she ever let herself become involved in this mess? She wasn't used to such complicated affairs and their crosscurrents of love and hate. She would have said ordinarily that she was fair at separating fact from falsehood. Now she seemed to have lost her bearings. She could no longer tell what she knew from what she believed, what she believed from what she wanted to believe.

If she had any sense, she would make some excuse to pack her suitcase and be gone, not only from the lodge and Snowmass, but from Colorado. Coming here had been a mistake on several accounts. Not only had she landed herself in this situation, there had been precious little opportunity to think seriously about her future. Even now, in the middle of the night, she could not make her mind settle to the task.

The lodge was quiet. There had been no raised voices or slamming doors for some time. The abrupt sound of a knock was startling in the stillness. Clare hesitated an instant, uncertain whether the summons had been at her own door or from somewhere nearby. Flinging back the cover, she slipped into her robe of turquoise fleece and went to see.

The balcony outside her room was empty. She was just about to step back inside when she heard the sound of a door closing. The knock had been near, all right, next door, in fact. Just before the panel snapped shut, there had been the sound of a voice, a woman's voice. Janine had been as good as her word. She had found a way to speak to Logan.

Clare, her face cold with distaste, started back inside once more. At that moment, she heard the slam of another door from a lower floor, on the opposite side of the pool. The direction from which the sound had come touched off a suspicion in her mind. She moved quickly out onto the balcony and looked over the railing. Below her, Marvin Hobbs had emerged from his room and was striding toward the elevator. His face grim, he stepped inside. The doors slid shut, and the elevator car began its upward whine.

Clare did not stop to think. She whirled back into her room and swung the door shut. Running to the connecting door, she beat a furious tattoo on its woodgrained surface, snapping the lock open with one hand at the same time.

"Logan?" she called as loudly as she dared. "Let me in."

The door opened inward, and she tumbled into Logan's bedroom. Logan, his hair tousled and his robe wrapped around him, stared at her in surprise not unmixed with irritation. Janine stood back, her hands clenched at her sides her face twisted with fury as she glared at Clare.

"I . . . I'm sorry, Logan. I don't mean to interfere, but Marvin Hobbs is coming."

"He can't," Janine objected. "He was sound asleep when I left."

"He isn't now," Clare said succinctly. Hard on her words came a sharp knock.

Clare flung a quick look at Logan. In defiance of his frown, she stepped to his bed and sat down at the foot, curling her legs under her in an effort to look as if she had been there long enough to be comfortable.

Logan lifted a brow; then a ghost of a smile banished the hardness from his face. Running the fingers of one hand through his hair, he stepped to the door. Janine made a quick gesture, as if she would stop him; then she brought her hand down, throwing her shoulders back with all the pride of a martyr.

Hobbs was just raising his fist to pound on the door. He gave Logan a curt nod, pushed the panel wider, and stepped into the room.

"Why, Mr. Hobbs this is getting to be quite a party," Clare said, her voice even, deliberately soothing, though nerves quivered in the arm upon which she was resting.

"Clare!" the producer exclaimed.

"What did you expect?" his wife asked, her tone arch. "She *is* his fiancée."

Marvin Hobbs was a blunt realist; he was also a gentleman in his own way. "My apologies for the intrusion, Clare. This is getting to be a habit, one I can only regret. Logan, if I say it won't happen again, perhaps you will overlook it one more time."

Janine gave Logan no time to reply. "I am glad to see you have some manners, Marvin" she snapped. "It is more than I expected when you came barging in here."

"Yes," her husband replied, his tone grim. "Having made my peace with Logan, I am now going to ask you, my dear wife, why are you traipsing around all over the lodge in your nightgown?"

"Why . . . I came to see Clare, of course. I knocked on her door, and I suppose she must have heard from in here with Logan. She called me over to this room." It was not a bad effort for such short notice. From the smile that twisted Janine's mouth, she knew it.

"I wasn't aware of any emergency that made it necessary for you to pay Clare a visit so late – and so quietly."

Janine looked at her husband with loathing. "If you are referring to the way I left my room, I was trying not to wake the entire lodge. Excuse my courtesy. As to why I wanted Clare, before you forced your way in I was asking if she and Logan wanted to make a foursome for the long slope tomorrow morning. An inch of new powder is predicted overnight, and I am told Clare has improved to the point where she is capable of anything."

Her husband grunted. "I can't make it in the morning. I am expecting a call from the Coast."

"Too bad. Perhaps Clare and Logan and I –"

"I appreciate the invitation, Janine," Clare said hurriedly, "but I'm not in your league yet, and I know it. Besides, John says it would be foolish to attempt anything really tricky right now. If I get into a situation I can't manage and take a bad fall, all his good work might be for nothing, since it would set me back, ruin the small amount of confidence he has been able to instill. I think I had better stick to the intermediate slopes."

"I will stay with Clare," Logan said. "Of course, if you would care to join us, Janine, we have no objections." Moving to the bed, he sank down beside Clare. The extra weight on the mattress made her sway toward him, momentarily off balance. He reached out to catch her, drawing her comfortably against his side.

"No," Janine said, a shrill edge in her voice. "I graduated from such minor thrills long ago. I will leave them to you two. It was just an idea. I didn't want your Clare to think I feel too superior to ski with her. It has been a long time since I was an amateur, but I still remember how little I relished being left behind when everyone else was taking the long runs."

"It was thoughtful of you," Clare said. "Perhaps I can take you up on it at least once before it is time for me to go."

"Go?" Hobbs queried.

"Back to my home in Louisiana. I . . . I prefer not to become involved with Logan's life in California and his work as an actor just yet."

"I see. He will be a bigger fool than I think if he lets you out of his sight." The producer moved to hold the door, looking at his wife. "Shall we go?" he asked.

The last thing Janine Hobbs wanted was to leave Clare alone with Logan, and yet there was nothing else she could do, not with her husband's implacable stare upon her. Logan gave her no help, watching her with his face unyielding and the look in his eyes one of patience tried to the edge of endurance. Janine swung toward the door. The glance she threw at Clare as she stepped over the threshold held all the venom of her pent-up rage.

As the door closed behind the couple, Logan turned to Clare. "So you came to my rescue?"

"Yes," she said, her voice hard, "though I am not sure you deserve it." She tried to free her feet so she could stand up, only to discover that he was sitting on the hem of her gown and robe.

"What is that supposed to mean?"

"You know very well. If you were half as concerned about your screenplay as you pretend, you would never have let Janine into your room." Sparks of anger glittered in her gray eyes as she tugged at her robe.

Logan made no move to free her. "What was

180

I supposed to do? Leave her standing outside banging on my door to wake the dead?"

"I don't see why not," Clare snapped. "It would certainly have given her husband a better idea of what is supposed to be going on."

He gave a sigh of exasperation. "If I had known Marvin was on her heels, I might have let her hammer away. Unfortunately, I didn't know it, and I had the strange idea that the fewer people who learned of her nocturnal ramblings, the better it would be."

"The better for whom?" she asked, her tone laced with sarcasm.

Abruptly he caught her shoulders, stilling her twisting efforts to release herself, turning her to face him. "What is the matter with you? I didn't invite Janine up here, if that's what you are thinking."

"No, I know you didn't. You weren't trying to get rid of her, either."

"How was I to do that? Pick her up bodily and throw her out."

"You could have used some of that fine contempt and lack of welcome you had ready when I landed on your doorstep a few days ago."

He stared at her, a considering look in his blue eyes. "Does that still rankle?" he asked quietly.

"Not at all," she denied. Her tone was

impatient, but she refused to look at him, staring fixedly at the hollow of his throat.

"If that isn't it, then what is on your mind? You wouldn't be just a little jealous, would you?"

"Jealous!" Her head came up. "You flatter yourself Logan Longcross."

His eyes narrowed. "Small chance of that, with you freezing every time I come near you. I hope if you ever have a real fiancée you don't avoid his touch the way you have avoided mine lately. You do, and I can promise the engagement won't last long. If you think my reaction to Janine's midnight visit harmed the chances of the project, I will have to tell you that your attitude toward me is not doing it any good, either."

"If you are talking about this evening," Clare said, her anger making her careless, "Janine was watching."

"What does that have to do with anything?" he demanded.

"Everything," she said, then stopped, uncertain of the wisdom of her impulse to throw Janine's duplicity in his face, unsure of how the subject should be approached even if she should decide to go on.

"Out with it," Logan grated, giving her a small shake.

"All right," she said on a deep breath. "Janine came to see me after she overheard us the other night. She has guessed what we have been up to. She agreed not to make a fuss, since she took the whole thing as a compliment to her. She was willing to put up with the farce so long as I did not try her patience too much by allowing you to . . . to make love to me in public."

Logan stared at her a long moment. Finally he said, "I see. And you told her she was right?"

"No, but since she threatened to go to her husband with the tale if we became to. . . . too intimate, I had to do as she said."

"Without consulting me?"

"Janine said . . . that is, from the way she spoke, I assumed you already knew what she thought, and what she wanted."

"You mean you assumed I had led her to believe that all this with you was for her sake. Go on, don't spare my feelings. You took every word she said for the truth, didn't you?"

"What does it matter what I believed?" Clare said a shade desperately. "It has nothing to do with me. But you can see I had no choice but to take Janine at her word when she said she would jeopardize everything if I played up to you."

"It never occurred to you that by doing as she said, you were practically admitting she was right?"

"It did, but what did it matter, so long as she kept quiet until Marvin Hobbs had signed to do the screenplay for you?"

"You worked all that out for yourself without telling me, without giving me fair warning that Janine might come charging up to my room expecting me to reassure her of heaven knows what?"

There had been reasons for that, reasons rooted in her doubts of his character. She did not intend to go into them, not now. Clare said nothing.

Logan went on. "I doubt that it is possible to repair the damage completely, but if the occasion arises, I intend to try. I would like to be able to count on your cooperation. Do you think you could bring yourself to be a little more accommodating in the future?"

"Accommodating? What do you mean by that?"

"Since you have to ask," he said, a dry note in his voice, "it might be best if we tried a little practice to familiarize ourselves with the scene, and each other."

His eyes were compelling as he drew her to him. He slipped his arms behind her, holding her close. His lips touched hers with fire, setting the blood racing in her veins. The grip of his left hand loosened, and he touched her cheek with the tips of his fingers, trailing down the tender curve of her neck to the opening of her robe.

Clare wanted to resist, to hold herself aloof from such an obvious appeal to her senses, but as his kiss deepened and his firm, sure touch brought its response, she felt herself drowning in a languorous weakness. She was pressed closer and closer, until her body seemed near to merging with his, and still she was not close enough. His mouth explored the moist corner of her lips and slid with sensuous heat over the smooth angle of her jawline.

"Logan . . ." she breathed in a soft protest as his head dropped lower, brushing a warm caress along the tender curve of her neck, and lower still as her robe fell away to expose her silk-clad breasts.

Lifting a hand, she touched the golden crispness of his hair. He went still, holding a deep-drawn breath. The tightly suspended seconds ticked past. Slowly, by careful degrees, he began to breathe again, and Clare sighed. With a gentle sureness Logan released her, though the effort it cost him was as plain as it was controlled. His face rigid, he closed her robe over her nightgown and tightened the belt once more.

Getting to his feet, he reached for her hand and pulled her to a standing position. A long strand of her hair lay curling across the lapel of her robe. He picked it up and smoothed it back over her shoulder. His attention on what he was doing, he said, "That wasn't such a good idea after all. Whoever it was meant to help, it seems to have backfired."

The regret in his voice was clear. If he thought she was overly affected by his casual caresses, she would disabuse him of the notion. "It doesn't matter," she said, her voice as quiet and composed as she could make it.

He frowned, then turned abruptly to stride to the connecting door. Pulling it open, he stepped back. "In that case," he said, "all you need to do is remember the lesson."

"I intend to," Clare answered, her gray eyes wide and dark as she stepped into her bedroom. As the door swung shut behind her, she turned and deliberately clicked the lock into place.

That done, she moved to the window and drew back the draperies. The night was dark and still. The only light came from a mercury-vapor streetlamp some distance away. Around its pale, red-tinged globe could be seen the swirl of snow flurries as the new powder Janine had mentioned came down to cover the ground.

A shudder ran over the surface of Clare's skin. It was the snow, she told herself. Just looking at it made her cold. The chill desolation she felt had nothing to do with Logan Longcross or what had passed between them. She was not so without sense as to be affected by anything he might do or say. Falling in love with him was the last thing she would think of doing.

The only think was, love did not need thought. It only required feeling.

What was she to do? The answer was simple. She would do her best to conceal what she felt, knowing full well the hopelessness of it. Logan, so self-contained and solitary, would not appreciate this added complication.

What kind of woman would it take to touch his heart, to penetrate the icy layers of protection with which he had surrounded it? Would it be, despite his denials, someone like Janine?

Clare turned away from the window, moving toward the bed. What did it matter? she asked herself. Soon she would be gone. It was nothing to her, nothing at all. And yet, even as she tried to convince herself, she knew she lied.

9

The snow was still falling the next morning, dropping gently from a heavy gray-white sky with tireless persistence. Due to the dimness inside her room and her restless night, Clare slept late. Logan was already in the coffee shop, a newspaper spread before him and a cup of coffee in his hand, when Clare descended for breakfast.

He looked up at her approach. Folding his paper, he tossed it to one side. "Good morning," he said, his manner no different from any other morning.

Clare returned his greeting and took the chair he held for her. As he seated himself across from her once more and picked up a menu, she said, "You haven't eaten?"

"No, I was waiting for you."

"You didn't have to do that."

"I wanted to," he answered, his tone so firm she was left with nothing to say.

It was not a comfortable meal. The events of the night before hovered between them like another presence at the table. They spoke of the weather and of the skiers that poured from the lodge onto the slopes, undaunted by the flakes as dry and light as down drifting from the sky. When the waiter brought their order, Clare made a pretense of eating, pushing at her ham omelet and taking small sips of juice. Logan glanced once or twice at her pale face, then put down his fork.

"What with one thing and another, I don't think I thanked you for what you did last night," he said. "I am grateful for the concern that made you come to my aid."

"It . . . it seemed a shame for the chances of the script to be spoiled after all your efforts," she replied, her attention centered on the corner of toast she was spreading with jam.

"I understand well enough that your thoughts were for the project, not for me," he answered.

At the dry tone of his voice, she looked up. "I did have some concern for you," she said. "Irate husbands have been known to shoot, and otherwise dispose of, the men who get too close to their wives."

"You would be distressed if I were . . . disposed of in some way?" he asked, leaning back in his chair.

Clare gave him a wide-eyed stare. "Of course. I mean, look at the fix I would be in, pretending to be your fiancée, cozily settled in the room next to yours. How would it look to the outsiders who would be called in? Anyway, I have this terrible feeling that if you were to meet your doom, I would wind up being blamed for it – the woman scorned, or some such nonsense."

"Little devil," he said softly.

There was a light in his dark blue eyes Clare had never seen before. She looked down at her plate. "I don't mean to be unfeeling, but you would be in no shape to be of any help to me."

His voice solemn, he answered, "Yes, I can see that. Am I to understand you weighted all these frightening possibilities before you came charging into my room last night?"

"Well, no," she said, tilting her head. "At the time, I relied solely on my instinct for self-preservation."

"Don't you think it may have been just a little overworked lately?"

"You mean because it has had to get me through several sticky, not to say embarrassing, situations with you?"

"No, darling Clare, because it doesn't seem to be warning you of the risk you are running right this minute!"

The spontaneous endearment and the smile that went with it affected Clare so strangely that she sat unmoving for an instant; then, with an effort she forced a laugh at the threat.

"Very wise," Logan said when she made no comment. Picking up his coffeecup, he drained it, then set it down. "What would you like to do this morning? Stay in? Go for a drive?"

Staying at the lodge before the fire sounded pleasant, but it was almost certain to mean time passed in the company of Janine and Marvin. Seeing them again would have to come eventually, though she preferred to put it off as long as possible. A drive would serve the purpose nicely, if it were not for the fact that it would mean long hours with Logan, hours that would be far from comfortable, given her newfound knowledge. Another time, she might have made her excuses and driven out to spend the morning with Bev, but this was her friend's day for volunteer work at the hospital.

"We could try the slopes as Janine suggested last night," Clare said at last.

"Feeling intrepid, are you?"

"The snow is what people come here for, isn't it?"

"Definitely," Logan answered, and signaled for the waitress approaching just then with a steaming coffeepot to bring the check instead.

They left the lodge a short while later. The distance to the ski lift was not great. They set out on foot, their boots clumping with a hard, icy sound on the paved walkway, and their breaths fogging in the chill air. Glancing back, Clare could see smoke rising from the chimney of the lodge, joining the blue-gray pall from the other chimneys all over the resort. The smell of it hung in the air, mingling with the tang of the evergreens. The windows of the lodge coffee shop looked out on this side. Clare thought she saw Janine at one of the tables near the glass, staring fixedly in their direction. She could not be certain. It might have been any woman transfixed by the familiar face of the blond actor beside her. Most of the people staying at the lodge had grown used to seeing him, but there were a few arrivals every day who had to overcome the shock.

The waiting line at the lift was fairly long, but it was a cheerful and friendly crowd. As they stood waiting, men in rust-colored parkas marked with gold crosses on their backs walked along the queue. Their smiles were cordial and polite, though once they took a skier aside. After a brief consultation, the man headed back in the direction of the lodge.

Clare had seen the men in the rust parkas at a distance several times before, but she had never seen them at the lifts. "What is it?" she asked Logan in an undertone. "Who are those men, and what are they doing?"

"They are members of the ski patrol. They are checking for safety straps. That's the strip of leather attaching your ski to your leg in case you come out of your bindings in a fall. If it's not there, your ski runs off downhill by itself, a danger to other people on the slopes."

"They are sort of police, then?"

"Not exactly, though they have a good bit of authority. Some are professionals, others are volunteers, good skiers with special training who give their time to keep other people out of trouble, and help them when they are unlucky enough to get into difficulties."

"They sound like nice people to know."

"Yes," Logan answered. "Here's the lift. Up we go."

Above them, the top of Snowmass Mountain was lost in the low-hanging snow clouds. The thick white mist coiled around the crest, obscuring the tops of the slopes. Riding upward into it was eerie, and at the same time fascinating.

Logan was first off the lift, though Clare was

close behind. He waited until he knew she was ready, then pushed off. She followed immediately in his tracks, trying to match his form and style, taking the same turns. He glanced back at her once or twice, flashing a grin beneath his ski goggles. Deep in concentration, Clare did not attempt to return it; still, she appreciated his close watch.

At the foot of the slopes they came to a stop in a spray of deep snow. "Again?" Logan asked.

"Again," Clare answered, her eyes bright and her lips, red from exercise and the cold, curving in a smile.

Their second run was a carbon copy of their first. On the third, Clare decided not to follow so closely. She would use Logan's parallel tracks to guide her, but she would try for a few independent moves if it looked and felt right. Off the lift, she waited until Logan was several feet ahead of her, then shoved away down the run.

The surge of exhilaration she felt was indescribable. Her skis were running free and yet controlled. The wind was in her face, and snow swirled around her, wafted by the force of her passing. She was alert and agile, ready for anything. Logan was a swift-moving form before her, one it seemed she could catch with a little extra effort. She flew past a skier practicing the twisting, natural stop to one side of the slope. She knew other skiers were coming down behind her in a plunge for the bottom of the hill, but she had no time to think of them. All that mattered was her own speeding progress.

From the top of the slope there came a shout ringing with anger. Seconds later, Clare heard the rush of a fast-moving skier, someone hurtling down the slope like a racer. She held her pace with care.

Suddenly there came a flash of orange in front of her as the skier cut directly across her path. Clare could not prevent herself from flinching, throwing herself off balance, and then, as she fought to recover, she felt her ski pole torn from her grasp, caught by the pole of the other skier.

Clare went down in a spinning, tumbling fall. Pain wrenched at one ankle as she heard the bindings of her skis snap open, and then she was sliding facedown in the cold drifts of snow.

What happened then was confusing as Clare tried to regain her breath that had been forced from her lungs by the fall, and yet the voices of the people gathering around her, talking excitedly, were clear.

"I saw it, man! That crazy idiot in the orange

suit nearly knocked me down getting off the lift, then went barreling down here and ran right over the girl."

"You mean on purpose?"

"Sure I mean on purpose. What do you think, somebody is going to hit two different people and still be standing up, flying away, if they didn't mean to do it?"

"Where did they go?"

"Right on down the hill, just like nothing happened — or like they didn't mean to get caught at the scene."

"You got a good look at him?"

"Ski mask, orange coveralls, not very big. Either a teenager or a woman. Hard to tell in this kind of weather."

"Somebody ought to go for the ski patrol."

"Bright idea, except somebody already took care of that chore five minutes ago."

"Where are those guys, then?"

"They'll get here. Have to bring the toboggan, you know, to take her down. Won't move her without it."

"Is she hurt bad?"

"I don't know. Afraid to turn her over to see."

"It wouldn't hurt to let her breathe," came the sharp-edged rejoiner.

Clare felt gentle hands turning her head and shoulders.

"If she has a broken neck, I never touched her!"

"That's great, just great."

"Say, that's the girl with Logan Longcross. What do you want to bet heads roll over this — starting now. Here he comes.

The voices receded. Clare felt her shoulders lifted, heard Logan speak her name. His warm fingers closed around her gloved hand.

She opened her eyes. "I'm all right," she said. "Just . . . just . . ."

"Don't try to talk, darling."

"No, really," she protested, trying to turn.

"Lie still and be quiet," he said, his hold tightening.

Clare, mulling with slow wonder the harsh, ragged sound of his voice and the lack of color underneath the deep tan of his face, obeyed.

She *was* all right, however. When the ski patrol delivered her to the first-aid station and she was examined, the attending doctor found no more than a sprained ankle, mild shock, and facial abrasions. Bed rest for the remainder of the day and an early night were recommended, along with a sedative and a wrapping for the ankle. Starting the next day, she could do as she pleased, go anywhere she could manage to hobble with crutches — or anywhere she could persuade some man to carry her. The doctor, a jovial gentleman with graying hair and beard, seemed to think, as he cast a look at Logan sitting anxiously beside her, that the last would be no problem.

The doctor was a fair prophet. Logan, refusing the offer of an ambulance to deliver Clare back to the lodge, carried her in his arms to his car that he had ordered brought to the aid station. With no sign of effort, he transferred her from the car all the way to her room. He left her alone while she made ready for bed, returning a short time later with a glass of ice-cold water with which to take the prescribed sedative

Clare expected him to go away then. Instead, he settled into one of the armchairs and sat staring out the window.

Clare lay watching his shadowed profile for long moments. At last she said quietly, "You don't have to stay."

"I know."

"There is no need at all."

He did not answer, nor did he show any sign of moving.

"It . . . it wasn't your fault, you know. There was nothing you could have done to prevent it."

"Wasn't there?" An unaccustomed note of bitterness sounded in his voice.

"No, there wasn't. I . . . I am sorry if this interferes with the signing of the contract."

"It isn't going to. Don't think about things like that. Don't think about anything at all. You are supposed to be resting."

"How can I, when this changes everything? I'm no more use to you now. I may as well go home."

"And give up?" he queried softly, showing no impatience for the fretful tone of her voice.

"It's not that," Clare answered, trying to banish her disappointment, to think only of what was best for Logan. "I just don't want to be in the way."

"You won't be. You can leave, if that's what you want, and I wouldn't blame you for getting out when you can, but I hope you will stay. I need you, Clare, you and no one else."

There was something more than satisfactory in that speech. Clare wanted to pursue it, but she was growing sleepy. In spite of her efforts, her brain refused the task. She closed her eyes, contenting herself by murmuring. "If you are sure."

"I am," he replied, his voice reaching her as from a great distance.

She started to smile, then stopped as she felt a twinge of soreness in her face. The skin of her cheek was sticky with the thick layer of ointment the doctor had applied. She wanted to ask for a tissue to remove a portion of it, but the words would not come. Her eyelids lifted a fraction. Logan still sat near the window, his face somber as he stared at nothing. Clare frowned a little; then her lashes fluttered down and were still.

10

"Your flowers are absolutely gorgeous," Beverly said as she leaned over Clare, carefully applying an antibiotic ointment to the scraped place on her cheek.

"The roses are from Logan. The cinerarias came from Janine and Marvin just a little while ago."

"I might have guessed," Beverly replied, casting a wry look in the direction of the flower stand in one corner of the room. Though pretty in themselves, the pot of vivid purple cinerarias clashed painfully with the full bouquet of red roses.

Clare smiled, though there was a shadow in the depths of her gray eyes.

Observing it, Beverly changed the subject. "The doctor didn't mention the possibility of scarring, did he?"

"On my face, you mean? No, it's just a snow burn, nice and clean. He said it should clear up in a few days."

"I thought as much; I just wanted to make sure you weren't worried about it."

"Heavens, no," Clare said, laughing up at her friend. "I know very well that my beauty will return and I shall walk again someday. The only problem is, how I am going to keep myself occupied until then?"

"Bored already, after only one day?"

"Three-quarters of a day."

"Well, it serves you right," Beverly said, getting to her feet and returning the cap to the tube of ointment. "You should not have been out on the slopes without your expert instructor."

"I had to try it without him sometime; he can't go around skiing with me all my life. I don't believe, friend or not, that you would stand for that. Besides, I wasn't exactly alone."

"No, and I have a feeling that was half the problem."

"I hope you won't say so in front of Logan. He already feels responsible enough for my accident. Why, I can't imagine, because that is all it was, an accident. There wasn't a thing he could have done to prevent it. If anyone is to blame, I am. The other skier wouldn't have tried to cut in front of me if I had been following Logan as close as I should."

"No, and furthermore, he might have recognized her, which would not have done at all."

"What are you saying?" Clare asked.

"I think you know well enough. I've heard the description of this hit-and-run skier, and I've taken the measure of Mrs. Janine Hobbs, a lady who has cut quite a figure on the slopes lately with her European outfits and her snobbery. It wouldn't surprise me to learn Logan is responsible for the fall you took, at least indirectly. Janine has not been at all happy with the attention he has been paying to you these last few days."

The same thought had occurred to Clare, though it was hard to make herself believe anyone could set out deliberately to injure a person for such a petty reason. "Why? She knows there is nothing serious between Logan and me."

"She did warn you about getting too cozy. I don't suppose she could have had any occasion for thinking you were ignoring her warning?"

Clare slanted a long glance at her friend. "Are you asking if Logan and I are getting cozy?"

"No!" Beverly exclaimed. "What you do is your own business."

"I take that to mean that you think we are."

The other girl moved to sit on the foot of the bed where Clare lay. "No, not really. But I can't help but be worried about you all the same. When is it all going to end, Clare? How is it going to end?"

Clare could not meet her friend's concerned gaze. "I don't know," she said, smoothing the ribbon trim of the blanket that lay across her lap. "I wish I did."

"You don't have to stay, you know. You can always pack up and leave. I could help you get everything together right now, and in a little while John could come and carry you to the car."

"Oh, Beverly, I appreciate the offer, but I can't go and leave everything unsettled, Leave Janine a clear field. There is no telling what kind of scheme she will come up with next for entangling Logan in some sordid mess."

"You are worrying about Logan when you should be worrying about yourself. What bothers me is why he is putting up with all this. I would have sworn he wasn't the type to let himself be manipulated in any way, not by a woman like Janine."

"It's the screenplay. He wants Marvin to do it."

"Is that it? Is it really? It seems like a high

price to pay to me, especially for someone like Logan, though I may be making the classic mistake of thinking the actor is the man. Anyway, I want you to know that if anything else happens, you are to come to me on the double. Don't think twice, don't look back, just come. All right?"

"You are sweet for putting up with me, when this was supposed to be a holiday with you."

"I am not sweet," Beverly declared, reaching out to touch Clare's hand with firm, reassuring fingers. "I am a sour and jealous pessimist, and I probably shouldn't be worrying you with all this. Maybe I should go on home and take my frustrations out on John. It may not be fair, but he did ask for it when he asked me to marry him."

"I expect he would feel slighted if you took your problems to anyone else."

"Yes, and he will also feel slighted if he doesn't find his dinner waiting. It's getting to be that time."

So it was. Beyond the windows, night was closing in, though the transition from the dull gray of the snow clouds to darkness had been so gradual Clare had not noticed. Beverly gathered up her coat and handbag, gave Clare a quick hug, then moved to the door.

With her hand on the knob she said, "Take

care of yourself Clare, and remember what I said."

"Yes, I will," Clare promised, and gave a final wave as Beverly let herself out into the hall. She lay listening to Beverly's receding footsteps. Her thoughts, as she stared at the flowers, the red roses and purple cinerarias across the room, were somber, as dark and as cold as the night beyond the windows.

It might have been a few minutes, it might have been an hour later, when a knock came on the other door. It had locked automatically behind Beverly. Clare was just pushing back the covers when the panel swung open and Logan entered. He smiled at her surprise and pulled a key from the lock.

"Passkey," he said. "I didn't see any reason why you should have to get up." Stepping to one side, he waved in a waiter pushing a wheeled table laden with covered dishes.

"What is this?" Clare asked, by no means certain she liked this invasion of her room while she was dressed only in her gown and robe.

"Dinner," Logan answered.

That was not quite the full explanation. The table that was pushed close to her bedside held china and silver for two, and the waiter, before he whipped the covers from the array of dishes, pulled up an extra chair and positioned it across from Clare. That done, he went out and returned with a portable wine cooler. Opening the bottle, he poured a small amount in one of the glasses on the table and handed it to Logan. Logan tasted it and gave a nod. The waiter half-filled the companion glass on the table, then poured a like amount into Logan's glass before returning the bottle to its cooler.

"Will that be all?" the young man asked.

Yes, thank you." Logan dropped a bill into his hand, and moved to close the door behind him. Turning with a disarming grin, he said to Clare, "I hope you don't mind. I thought it would look odd if I left you up here to eat alone. Besides, I was in no mood for a three-some with Marvin and Janine."

"I see," Clare said. "No, of course I don't mind, though if I had known, I would have dressed for the occasion."

"I know. That's why I didn't tell you. Not," he added hastily, "that I wanted to catch you at a disadvantage. I just didn't want you to go to any extra effort. We ought to know each other well enough by now to dispense with that kind of formality — even if it wasn't for your ankle."

Moving to the table, he picked up Clare's wineglass and placed it in her nerveless fingers. The smile he gave her as he touched the rim of his own to hers was warm and without reserve.

"How do you feel?" he asked when Clare had sipped at her wine.

"Fine," Clare answered, "but as if too much fuss is being made over nothing."

"I wouldn't call it nothing," Logan objected.

Clare gave a slight lift of her shoulders. "Everybody takes a fall or two when learning to ski. I feel lucky to have come out of it with nothing more serious than a sprain."

"Yes," Logan agreed, staring down at the wine in his glass as he swirled it slowly around the rim.

When he did not go on, Clare asked, "What do we have to eat?"

"Steak and potato. Not inspired, but at least I know you like it." He looked up with a grin. "It can't be as good as the charred steak and burned potatoes we cooked in the fireplace at the house, but I decided against asking the kitchen to duplicate that feast. I expect they would have thought I was crazy."

"It's possible," Clare answered, a slow smile rising in her gray eyes.

Logan held her gaze for a long moment; then he glanced down at the table. Draining his glass, he took his place before her. "We had better eat," he said, his voice carefully casual, "before everything gets cold."

Clare had done nothing to confine her hair as

she lay all day in bed. It spilled over her shoulders in golden strands, curling against her neck and down across her breasts. Once she glanced up to find Logan watching her holding a forkful of avocado salad in midair. The strangeness of having him there in her room brought a flush of color to her cheeks. His interest was also disturbing. This evening he wore beige slacks with a beige-and-blue sports shirt. He looked relaxed, at home in his surroundings, and yet there was something about his manner that made Clare feel flustered and aware of a need to be on her guard. She had not seen him since earlier that morning, when he had settled her in her room with a sedative. His concern then had been comforting, but she had not expected it to last.

"Isn't this better than eating alone?" Logan asked, breaking in on her thoughts.

"Yes, though if you don't stop pampering me, I am going to be hopelessly spoiled when this is over. I haven't thanked you for the roses. They are beautiful." Red roses were usually for love. No doubt he had sent them because it was what people would expect of a fiancée. It could not hurt to pretend, just a little, could it?

"I'm glad you like the roses. As for the rest, it's little enough after this morning."

Clare looked down at her plate, then looked

up again. "About this morning, could I ask you something?"

"Anything."

"Did you see anything of the skier who caused me to fall? I mean, he — or she — whoever it was, came down the slope behind you."

Logan put down his fork. "I saw the skier, yes. But he veered off from where I came to a stop. His face was covered — goggles, ski mask, cap pulled down over his hair. I didn't really know what had happened. I looked back, and you were down, then this skier came flying past. I was more interested in getting back up to you just then than the other person, especially since I didn't know he had caused your fall."

"He? Are you certain it was a man?"

"No," he said almost reluctantly, "I'm not."

"It could have been a woman, then? Could it even have been Janine?"

"I didn't mean to disturb you with it, if you were willing to accept the theory that your fall was an accident, but as long as you have guessed, then I will say the skier was almost certainly Janine. I wouldn't like to swear to it, considering the weather conditions and the way she was dressed, but styles of skiing are fairly distinctive. The equipment she was using was standard rental stuff, not her European boots and skis, but the size was about right, and then there is the suspicious way she gave me a wide berth. Why would she do that unless she was afraid of being recognized despite her disguise?"

"But why? Why would she want to harm me?"

"She wasn't too happy with the way you turned the tables on her in my room the other night."

Clare gave a nod. "And she wasn't too thrilled, either, with the way you opted to come with me on the lower slopes instead of taking one of the long trails with her this morning." There had also been Janine's warning to stop throwing herself at Logan in public, though Clare did not see any reason for bringing that up again.

"I expect she meant to embarrass you by making you take a spill. Unfortunately, she cut it too fine."

Clare, remembering the way her pole had been jerked from her hand, could not agree. Janine Hobbs had meant to hurt her if she could. The producer's wife would have shed few tears if Clare had broken her neck. That anyone could wish her harm, even in the form of a serious accident, was so unbelievable to Clare that she could not quite bring herself to put it into words.

"Does Janine realize you suspect her?" she asked after a long pause.

"I haven't mentioned it to her, if that is what you mean," Logan answered, "but I think she knows. She didn't say a word when I told her I was dining with you this evening, and it was not because Marvin was present. We were alone."

"I suppose some good came from this morning, then," Clare said with an attempt at lightness. If Logan had looked at Janine with the contempt burning in his blue eyes that Clare saw there now, she did not wonder that the woman had not tried to detain him. Abruptly an idea surfaced in Clare's mind. Circling it cautiously, she was not certain if she dared put it into effect. What Logan would say, she could not imagine, but it was always possible that he might not find out. Deep in thought, she fell silent.

"Would you like desert?" Logan asked when Clare leaned back on her pillows and dropped her napkin beside her plate.

Clare shook her head. "I couldn't."

"Help me finish the last of the wine, then."

Watching as he rolled the table aside, poured wine into her glass, and handed it to her once more, Clare said, "Are we celebrating some-thing?"

"I wondered when it was going to dawn on you."

"There was always the possibility that you were plying me with drink for nefarious reasons. I thought I would wait and see what you meant to do."

"One day," he said slowly, "you are going to joke your way into a dangerous situation. But not tonight."

Conscious of something suspiciously like the pique of disappointment, Clare said, "So what are we celebrating?"

Instead of answering, he walked to the con-necting door, unlocked it, and went into his own room. He returned a few seconds later carrying a manuscript. This he brought and dropped into Clare's lap.

Clare gathered up the pages in one hand. It was his screenplay, though it was no longer bound. "What is it? What have you done?"

"Made a few changes," he answered, taking up a position on the foot of her bed. "They are not hard to find, if you know where to look."

For a long moment Clare held his gaze; then she sat up straight and without ceremony handed her wineglass to Logan to hold. She flipped through the pages, scanning a few lines here, a few there. At last she looked up.

"You have changed your women," she said in wonder.

He laughed. "You make me sound like a sheik."

"You know what I mean," she said, waving the manuscript at him in an impatient gesture.

"Yes, I do. Do you like them better now?"

"Oh, yes, much. But why?"

"I decided after sober reflection that you were right; my female characters lacked strength. If they were going to behave the way I showed them during a crisis, they would never have lasted on the frontier, and if the women of the Old West had been weak, where would we all be now?"

"It's not only that," Clare said earnestly. "Both brothers in your script, at one point, fall in love with the same girl. The most intelligent and honorable of them makes great sacrifices to win her, while the other brother, for all his greed and weakness, displays the finer side of his nature to her. If she is a silly, vain, clinging little thing, it just doesn't make sense!"

"No, it certainly doesn't."

"She has to have some character, something besides a pretty face."

"She certainly does."

His ready acquiescence brought Clare up

short. She stared at him with a frown between her eyes. "Why are you being so agreeable?"

Her suspicion seemed to amuse him, for a laugh broke from him. His only answer was to hand her back her glass, however. "To women of character," he said, and drank, laughter gleaming in his blue eyes as he watched her.

He did not linger after that. She needed to rest, he said, but Clare thought the constraint that came between them following his mocking toast also had something to do with it. Taking the remains of their meal with him so she would not be disturbed by the waiter when he came for the table, Logan had gone into his room. A short time later, Clare thought she heard him go out, seeking livelier company, she supposed. She gave her pillow a hard thump, then allowed herself a wry smile for her petulance.

Hopping around on one foot, Clare washed her face, brushed her teeth, and made ready for bed. The jarring movement made her ankle throb. She thought that once she lay back down again, it would stop, but it did not. She tried to ignore the pain, to distract herself by reading. It didn't work.

At last she flung the covers aside and struggled to one foot again. She had a bottle of aspirin tablets with her, but it was on the dresser across the room. Clenching her teeth, Clare started toward them, though the pain of each hopping step brought a sick feeling into her throat. The deep-pile earth-brown carpet that covered the floor did not help matters. Its cushiony softness seemed determined to trip her.

Just as she reached the dresser, she stumbled and fell forward, catching the edge. The perfume, makeup, and sunscreen bottles that sat in a neat line on its surface fell with a rolling clatter. Clare grabbed for them and only succeeded in banging her elbow. The bottle of aspirin tablets skittered across the polished surface and toppled to the floor.

Clare took a deep, steadying breath; then, with grim determination in her eyes she worked her way around the end of the dresser and knelt with one hand outstretched toward the bottle.

At that moment the door behind her swung open. Swift footsteps crossed the carpet, then Logan went down on one knee beside her. His strong brown fingers closed around the bottle. He glanced at it, then swung to put it in her hand.

"Was this what you wanted?"

"Yes," Clare whispered.

"Why didn't you call me?"

"I . . . I thought I could get it. Besides, I was almost sure I heard you go out."

"Only for the evening paper," he said, indicating the folded newspaper beneath his arm. Placing his hands under her elbows, he helped her to her feet. "Are you in pain?"

"A little," she admitted.

He scanned her white face, then gave a nod. Tossing his paper onto the foot of the bed, he turned to the insulated carafe filled with ice and water that stood on a tray at the other end of the dresser. With economical movements he poured water into one of the plastic glasses provided by the lodge and handed it to her, then, taking the tablets from her, shook two of them into her hand. Face impassive, he watched as she swallowed them. Receiving the glass from her, he set it back on the dresser. Before she could guess his intention, he bent to catch her beneath her knees and lift her into his arms.

"Logan, no," she gasped. "You don't have to do this."

"Don't I?" he asked, his grip tightening.

Something in the low timbre of his voice affected her senses with a sweet languor. Though she knew she should protest, she did not care if he never let her go. Against all reason, against her will, she felt herself yielding to the planes of his body and the muscled hardness of his arms. Her body pliant, supple, she clung to him, the darkness of a confused and fearful longing shadowing her eyes.

Logan drew a deep breath, holding it constricted in his chest. The strong beat of his heart seemed to shudder through her, increasing the frantic pulsing of the blood in her own veins. He stared down at her, his gaze moving over the soft luster of her skin where it was not covered by the apricot silk of her gown. A muscle corded along the length of his jaw.

With sudden decision he leaned to place her on the bed. His lips brushed hers with gentle fire, and then he turned away. Picking up his newspaper, he left the room, closing the door quietly behind him.

She was grateful for his help, Clare told herself, and also for his restraint. It was a relief that he had not mistaken her weakness for an invitation. That did not explain the hot, silent tears that slid from the corners of her eyes, nor the feeling like the heaviness of despair that weighed her chest.

There was snow on the Plexiglas dome overhead, a white cover that made the open center of the lodge dimmer than usual. Now and then the melting snow, turned to slush by the warmth of the bright midmorning sun, would slide onto the roof, leaving a clear section of blue sky shining through like a piece of polished turquoise. The water in the heated pool beneath the dome lapped gently against the sides as Logan swam up and down with slow strokes. Clare, lounging in a cane chair filled with cushions, flipped through a magazine, pretending to read. Instead, she watched the man, memorizing the way his hair, sleek with water, molded to his head, the look of inward concentration he brought to what he was doing, and the smooth coordination of his muscled shoulders as his arms cleaved the water. It was a useless exercise, she knew, one that could bring her nothing but pain, now or in the future; still, she could not help herself.

At the sound of a door opening, Clare looked up. Janine and Marvin Hobbs were just emerging from the coffee shop at the far end of the pool. Marvin hailed Logan, then dragged up a chair and motioned him from the water. Logan heaved himself with a lithe movement to the side of the pool to sit relaxed with one arm resting on his knee. Marvin said something to Janine, and the woman glanced at Clare. The producer's wife nodded and made a laughing remark that made both men smile;

then, with conscious grace she moved along the side of the pool to where Clare lay.

"My dear Clare, we have been so worried about you – oh, your poor face!"

Self-conscious in spite of her intention to ignore Janine's gushing solicitousness, Clare raised a hand to her cheek. "It's nothing. It will be completely healed in a week."

"I do hope so. Such a pity if that silly little accident should leave you scarred. But as I was saying, Marvin and I have positively badgered Logan for news. We would have come to see you yesterday, but he would not hear of you being disturbed. I swear it is hilarious to think of him keeping people from you when so often they have had to be kept from him."

She would have to remember to thank Logan for the mercy of sparing her such a visit when she had been feeling her worst. "He has been good to me."

"I am glad to see you realize it, though I expect you are enjoying having a man like that at your beck and call, having him carrying you up and down like something precious on a pillow."

"Why? Because you would?" Clare asked, her tone tart.

"You are out of sorts this morning, aren't you?" Janine said with satisfaction. Looking around, she chose a tubular chair with green print cushions to complement her bright green dress and drew it up beside Clare's lounge.

"Not especially, all things considered," Clare replied.

Janine sent her an uncertain glance, smoothing her dress down over her knees. "You seem in an odd humor to me."

"Because I don't want your double-edged commiserations? How ungrateful of me! You will have to excuse me, I have other things on my mind, other things that just happen to concern you, Janine. I would like to have a few words alone with you as soon as it can be arranged."

"Alone? What on earth for?" The woman stared at Clare with her brows lifted in surprise, though there was an element of wariness beneath her poise.

"There is something I would like to discuss."

"What is the matter with here?" Janine asked, spreading her hands to indicate the open space around them.

"I would prefer not to be interrupted."

"And I would prefer not to be inconvenienced any more than is necessary. If you have something to say to me, then say it now."

Clare closed her magazine and put it to one side. "All right, if that's the way you want it.

What I wanted to speak to you about is my little accident, as you called it, only it wasn't an accident, as you are well aware."

"I haven't the least idea what you are talking about."

"I think you do. I am saying it was you on the ski slope yesterday, you who deliberately sliced in front of me, hoping to make me fall, making sure of it by snatching my pole when it looked like I might recover. There is no use denying it; you were recognized."

"You are lying!"

"No. And I would advise you to keep your voice down, unless you would like me to repeat my tale to your husband."

"He wouldn't believe you," Janine said, but the tone of her voice, much quieter than before, was an indication that she was far from sure.

"Possibly not," Clare conceded, hiding her sense of triumph. "I wonder if he would believe Logan."

"Logan? Logan recognized me?"

"So you admit it?" Clare asked quietly. Janine need not know that Logan was uncertain of her identity.

"Definitely not," Janine answered, but her eyes were harried as she turned to look at the two men at the end of the pool.

"It makes no difference. I am sure the police will be able to get to the bottom of the matter."

"The police!" Janine swung to face Clare, her face pale beneath the coating of her make-up.

"It is a question of assault, you see."

"You weren't touched," Janine declared, her eyes narrowing.

"Wasn't I? How do you know, I wonder, if you weren't there? The important thing, however, is that there was intent to cause physical harm, and there are any number of witnesses who can testify to that."

A cold smile curled Janine's mouth. "Quite the little lawyer, aren't you?"

"No, but my father was before his death."

"Then if you are so sure of your facts, why haven't you gone to the police already?"

The question was not expected. "I would have," Clare said with an air of candor, "but it could not help but be embarrassing. Logan would have to be dragged into it. Everything would come out – his relationship with you, why he came up here, how I came to be with him, your objections to my presence, your husband's jealousy, everything. The papers would have a field day, of course. I might have the satisfaction of seeing you brought to book, but at what cost? No, I feel sure there is some other way for this matter to be settled."

"And just what did you have in mind?" Janine inquired, her words cold and even with the rage that burned inside her.

"Surely you can guess," Clare said gently. "First of all, you will agree to leave Logan in peace. I think you know that if there ever was anything between the two of you, it is over now."

"Why, you —"

"Come on, Janine. Names won't hurt me," Clare said, impatience threading her voice. "In any case, that isn't all. I am also going to ask you to return to your husband's good graces. It will be to the advantage of all of us if you can manage to convince him there was no affair, that you were infatuated for a time and are now recovered. That shouldn't be too much to ask of someone who was once an actress."

"You must be crazy!"

"No, I don't think so. There is a reason for what I am saying. Once you have regained your husband's trust, you will encourage him, discreetly of course, to complete the arrangements to produce Logan's screenplay."

"That is blackmail," Janine said tightly.

"Yes, I believe it is. I think it might be more effective if I put a time limit on it, too. Shall we say that by the end of the week you will bring this business to a head?"

"That's impossible."

"I don't think so, not for someone of your . . . talents."

Janine stared at her with calculated rage. "If you think you can make me believe Logan is a party to this kind of underhanded trick, let me inform you I am not so stupid. He would never go through with it."

"No, he wouldn't, any more than he would take another man's wife. It's a good thing that I am the injured party, isn't it? If I go the police, I don't think Logan will ignore a subpoena, as much as he might like to."

"If I were to tell him what you are doing, I think he would put a stop to it."

This was a possibility Clare had not considered. She did not intend to let Janine know it, however. "He might try," she replied. "Then again, he might not. It is even possible he might be grateful."

"You would like that, wouldn't you?" Janine sneered. "That's the real reason you are doing this, because you are in love with him. Well, don't kid yourself, honey. You haven't got a prayer. If I can't have him, I can at least see to it that you don't either."

There was no time to go into the veiled

threat. At the far end of the pool, Marvin Hobbs was on his feet and Logan had reached to pick up his terry swim robe, wrapping it around himself. "Can I take it you intend to cooperate, then? I suggest you make up your mind, since the men are about to join us."

"Yes, damn you, I agree," Janine hissed, and turned toward Marvin and Logan, trying to arrange her features in a relaxed look of welcome.

Clare's smile was no less strained. She had won, and yet somehow the victory seemed incomplete. Now that it was over, it was incredible that Janine had actually believed she would go to the police. Only someone totally vindictive and uncaring of how she appeared in the press, could go through with such a thing. What had Janine meant by her statement that she could see to it Clare did not have Logan either? There was no point in worrying over it. Since she had no hope of Logan ever seeing her as anything more than a nuisance of a female reporter who was able to be of use in return for an interview, she had nothing to lose. Janine could not hurt her.

"What have you two girls been talking about?" Marvin Hobbs inquired.

"Nothing," Janine answered with a shrug. "Just this and that."

"Oh? Looked mighty interesting from where Logan and I sat."

Janine flicked a glance at Clare, then turned to her husband once more. "If you must know, we were talking about our two handsome men," she said with a small provocative smile. "I'm surprised the ears of both of you weren't burning."

Clare, finding Logan's blue gaze resting upon her with a query in its depth, felt the heat of a blush rising to her hairline.

11

The next three days passed without incident. Clare progressed from lying with her foot elevated to walking with aid. She spent a portion of the time rereading Logan's script, discovering that he had not only made the women characters stronger, but he had also softened the hard outlines of their personalities. She could take no credit for that change; still, it pleased her in some obscure way. Logan, when she had tried to express her approval, had only smiled at her with a quizzical look in his eyes.

He spent most of his time in her company, sitting with her, reading, talking, handing her whatever was out of reach, helping her to and from meals without the least sign of impatience. Such close attendance was probably because he felt responsible for what had happened, Clare told herself, but that did not prevent her from enjoying the easy companionship.

They were not troubled by Janine. Her time was taken up with her husband. With brittle gaiety and high spirits that seemed only barely under control, she enticed him out onto the slopes, cajoled him into taking her shopping in Aspen, or swept him with her for late hours at the nightspots around town.

Marvin Hobbs was kept so busy that there was little time for discussion of any kind between him and Logan. Clare was surprised that Logan did not chafe at the apparently permanent stall in the negotiations on his project. If it disturbed him, he did not show it.

Toward the end of the third day, as the two of them sat with feet stretched toward the fireplace in sole possession of the lounge, while the more energetic guests took to the snow, Clare looked at Logan. "When we were cooped up by the blizzard, you couldn't stand this confinement. You don't have to put up with it for my sake now, you know. I will be perfectly fine if you want to go out, maybe take advantage of the break in the weather."

"Are you, by any chance, trying to get rid of me?" Logan folded the section of the afternoon newspaper he was reading and let it sail to join the rest of the papers scattered on the floor around them.

"You know that isn't it. I just don't want you to feel you have to stay with me every minute."

"Oddly enough, I'm enjoying being lazy. I don't remember the last time I really relaxed. I think I must have been too keyed up; it always felt like I was wasting time when I wasn't out and doing, even if all I was doing was burning energy."

"Now that I have forced you into taking a rest, I suppose your career will go downhill from now on and you will blame me."

"I may at that," he answered, a smile flitting across his face.

"I didn't ask you to devote all your time to me," she pointed out.

"No, it was my own idea for a change. You are a restful person to be with, Clare. Did you know that?"

"Is that a compliment?" she asked suspiciously.

He did his best to look apologetic. "I think it must be."

"Then I will accept it," she said, "so long as you don't go to sleep."

"I don't think it's likely. There's no telling what you might do to attract my attention."

Clare turned slowly to face him, doubt shading her gray eyes. She had almost persuaded herself that he no longer believed she had wrecked her car to bring herself to his notice. As for the other incidents — her invasion of his room, her fall — surely he could not think there had been any kind of grandstand play for his attention in them.

Abruptly Logan reached out to touch her hand, his fingers closing warm and reassuring around hers. "No," he said, "I didn't mean it the way it sounded."

Clare summoned a laugh and a quick comment, and the moment passed, but the ease between them was gone. In its place was a stiff and self-conscious strain overlaid by unreasoning apprehension.

That fear, ill-defined but persistent, was still with Clare as she dressed for dinner. The shrilling of the telephone on the table beside her bed made her jump, spilling the makeup she was using to camouflage the marks on her face. They were fading, but a little flesh-colored makeup made them less conspicuous.

It was Marvin Hobbs who spoke when she lifted the receiver. He apologized for disturbing her at that time of day. Though knew it was an imposition, he would appreciate a few minutes of her time. There was a matter of importance he would like to discuss with her, alone, if she did not mind.

The request, and the blunt way that it was phrased, was so disconcerting that Clare found herself agreeing before she had time to think. The instant she put down the phone, she regretted it. She could not imagine what the producer would have to talk to her about; still less could she guess why he wanted to see her alone.

She was not given much time to consider the matter. Before she could take her robe from the closet and wrap it around her, he was knocking at the door.

Instinctively Clare sent a glance toward the connecting door into Logan's room. It was tightly closed. She thought he was in, but she could not be sure. Taking a deep breath, she slipped into her robe, wrapped the belt around her, and limped to answer the knock.

"I'm sorry," Marvin Hobbs said. "I know this is a bad time, but Janine is bathing and dressing for dinner just now, and it may be the only time I can talk to you without interference."

"It's all right," Clare said, sweeping her hair back with one hand as she gestured toward a chair. "Won't you sit down?"

The producer put a hand under her elbow to help her to an armchair, then took a seat across from her. "It's like this, Clare. I've never claimed to be the most intelligent man around, but I'm smart enough to know when I'm being given a snow job — if you will excuse the pun. My wife has been sweeter to me in the last three days than in the past three years, and while I won't deny it's been a nice change, it makes me wonder. The first question that comes to mind is, what does she want? This afternoon I found out."

"I don't see how that concerns me, Mr. Hobbs," Clare said.

"If you will bear with me, I will attempt to make it clear. You know that I flew up here expecting to find my wife with Logan, don't you?"

Clare, staring down at her hands in her lap, gave a reluctant assent.

"Janine swears to me there was nothing between the two of them except friendship, that the fact she happened to fly off in the same direction he did when the going got rough was strictly a coincidence. I don't mean to pry; still, I can't help wondering if Logan has given you an explanation of their relationship."

"He did mention it, yes."

"May I ask your opinion of what he told you?"

"My opinion? Why?"

"You do have a stake in this as Logan's

fiancée. I don't believe you are the kind of girl who would settle for a marriage based on lies."

Clare looked at Janine's husband, aware of the pain threading his tone. He was not enjoying his role as inquisitor, nor the necessity of speaking of his wife. There was only one answer to his question. She gave it. "Logan told me essentially the same thing as your wife told you."

"And you believe it?"

"I am satisfied that Logan is not in love with Janine and never had any intentions of meeting her here, if that is what you mean." As she spoke, Clare realized that in spite of Janine's insinuations, she believed exactly what she had said. If she could dismiss all idea of an affair between Logan and Janine, couldn't she also rid herself of the suspicion that he had tried to use the other woman to get what he wanted, just as he was using her?"

"I noticed you say nothing about what Janine might have felt for Logan."

Clare flicked him a brief glance. Logan had mentioned this man's intuition about people once. It had not been an idle observation. "I can't answer for her, of course."

"You think I should have some idea of my wife's feelings?" he suggested in recognition of her carefully neutral tone. "I think I do, Clare,

I think I do, and that is what troubles me." He got to his feet and moved to the window. Standing with his back to the room, he leaned with both hands on the sill.

Clare felt a little sick. She gripped her hands tightly together. "I don't understand."

"I told you I found out what Janine wants; she wants me to do this picture for Logan."

"I . . . So do I, Mr. Hobbs."

"Yes. You want it because that's what Logan wants. Isn't that it? You may admire the concept, but you have no personal ax to grind."

"I suppose so."

"Now, Janine, just a few days ago, was dead set against it. That was along about the time she came to Aspen. A week before, in L.A., she thought it was the greatest thing since *Gone with the Wind*. Don't misunderstand me. I love my wife, but I am not blind to her faults. I'm used to the way her mind works. I ask myself why she has been blowing hot and cold, and the reason I keep coming up with is you."

"Me?" The word was jerked from Clare by her surprise. She had thought that nothing short of clairvoyance could connect her to Janine's change of heart. It appeared she was wrong.

He swung around, crossing his arms over his chest. "Yes, you, Clare, and what Logan feels for you."

"What do you mean?" There was wariness in the look she gave him.

"First Janine likes the screenplay of Logan's then he leaves to come up here. She follows him, or so it looks to me, finds out about you, and immediately she hates the script, though she still wants to spend as much time as possible in the company of the man who wrote it. Then you have an accident caused by another skier. I happen to know Janine was on the slopes alone that morning, though when she came in she never said a word about what happened, just looked white and scared. Two days later she has a talk with you, and from that time on she acts like it's our second honeymoon. About the time I start to enjoy it, she begins to tell me how she has changed her mind again. She wants me to get serious about this project of Logan's. What am I supposed to make of it all?"

"What do you make of it, Mr. Hobbs?"

"I think," he said slowly, "that Janine wanted Logan, but he wouldn't play, because of his attachment to you, I think when she pushed him too far, he came up here to get away, and also to meet you. Janine didn't like the situation she found when she got here, and when she couldn't change it to suit herself, she let her temper run away with her common sense.

You were quick enough, and smart enough, to turn that to advantage, so Janine is now on your side."

"I am sure," Clare said slowly, "that you don't expect me to confirm any part of that."

"No, but I feel sure you would not have hesitated to deny it if there wasn't more than a little truth in it."

Clare let her gaze move to the door between her room and Logan's. She realized that by her silence she stood condemned. She had thought her scheme would help Logan; instead, it had put an end to the small chance that had been left. She lifted her chin. "I think you should know that Logan had nothing to do with . . . with Janine's recent change of heart. I don't believe he is even aware of it."

"I expected as much."

"I would rather he didn't find out, but I suppose that's too much to ask."

"No, I don't think so." Marvin Hobbs cleared his throat almost as if he were affected by the tears rising in her eyes. "You must love Logan very much."

Clare, her gaze held by his look of brooding concern, could only tell the truth. "Yes . . . yes, I do. I . . . May I ask what you mean to do now?"

"What I should have done in the first place,

consider this script of Logan's on its own merits. I doubt it will take me long to decide to do what I should have done weeks ago if it hadn't been for my own stubborn jealousy."

"You mean . . ."

"Exactly. I'm going to put the screenplay into production."

"Oh, Mr. Hobbs," Clare cried, coming to her feet.

"Careful there," he said, stepping forward to catch her arm as she swayed. "You don't want to put yourself out of commission before dinner. I want you and Logan to have dinner with us tonight. If you and he will come to my suite for a drink a little ahead of time, we can discuss it. I just happen to have a contract with me, brought along just in case. The terms are reasonable, since I don't expect Logan to accept anything less. We can sign it on the spot."

"I . . . don't know what to say," Clare said. "You are a generous man."

"Logan may not think so."

"That isn't what I meant."

"I know," Marvin Hobbs said, looking away as he moved toward the door. "You've been pretty generous yourself, all things considered. Logan is a lucky man. He's getting a fine girl. I hope he realizes it."

The door closed behind him. Clare stood staring at the wood-grain panel, trying to decide if the producer's words had more than their surface meaning. Could he suspect? Had Janine mentioned her suspicions to him? Surely not, or he would have said something. He had shown no reticence on anything else. Oh, but what did it matter so long as he produced Logan's screenplay?

Logan had won. She had won. After tonight, the purpose of this week with the producer and his wife would be finished. No doubt the party would break up. Janine and Marvin would go back to California. Logan too, more than likely. She would spend a few days with Beverly, letting her ankle mend, and then back to Louisiana. Back to ... whatever. Finally, once and for all, it would be over.

It would be over. The interlude would be finished. She would no longer be the fiancée of Logan Longcross. She would go through the days without seeing him, without speaking to him. His picture in magazines and newspapers would haunt her. She would torture herself watching his flickering image on the movie screen, knowing full well that though he seemed near, he was really thousands of miles away.

A few hours, that was all that was left. A few

hours, but already she could feel the pain of the parting beginning inside her. Not the least of it was knowing she herself had cut short the days they would have together.

Turning sharply from the door, Clare picked up a tissue from the dresser and began to repair the damage to her makeup caused by the tracks of her tears.

For dinner Clare wore the same long skirt and blouse of dusty rose that she had worn on that first night at the hotel. Removing the elastic bandage from her ankle, she buckled on a pair of high-heeled sandals. There was still some soreness in her foot, but she felt able to use it for short distances, even if she wasn't quite ready to dance or run. Her hair, freshly washed, she left in a shining mass on her shoulders. To put it up might give her a more sophisticated look, but that was not how she felt this evening. She felt vulnerable, out of her element, and much in need of some form of protective screen.

Logan, when he tapped on the connecting door and stepped into the room, had also returned to formal wear. After days of wearing nothing but casual clothing, he seemed like a stranger. It may have been a trick of the light, but she thought there was something withdrawn about his features as he turned to her.

"I see Janine called you," he said, nodding at her long dress. "I wanted to check and be sure you knew we were dining with her and Marvin, and tell you they are expecting us for a drink first."

"Yes, I know," Clare answered.

The temptation to ask if he knew Marvin Hobbs meant to bring to dinner a contract for the production of the screenplay was strong. However, there was always the possibility that he might resent her knowing before he did. In addition, there was no guarantee that Hobbs would not change his mind again before she and Logan could get downstairs.

"We don't have to go if you don't feel up to it," Logan said.

"I'm fine, really I am."

"Then why are you so pale? Did Marvin say something to upset you?"

"What?"

"I know he was here. I started to come earlier to ask you about dinner, but I heard voices, one of them male. It didn't take much in the way of detective work to find out it was Marvin."

"You spied on me?" Clare asked.

"I wanted to know who it was," he said with disarming simplicity. "Don't change the subject. What did Marvin want?"

"If you must know, it seems Janine has had a

change of heart and is now trying to get back into her husband's good graces. She told him there had never been anything between the two of you, and he was of two minds whether to believe her. He wanted to know what I thought."

"And what did you tell him?" There was a sound of tension in that quick question, despite the easy way Logan stood waiting for her answer.

"I told him you said much of the same thing, and that I trusted you, therefore I believed you."

"Was it the truth?"

Clare smiled, lifting one brow. "I think it must be. You had no reason to lie. At the time, you wanted nothing from me."

"Are you sure?" he queried.

"No, but what of it, so long as Marvin Hobbs thinks I am? If you expected to have some use for me, then you also offered something of yourself in return, so we are even."

For an instant Clare thought she saw a shadow of disappointment move across his face, and then he spoke. "So we are," he murmured. "A good way to leave it for now."

Had she imagined those last words? The promise they seemed to hold was tantalizing. As Clare, leaning on Logan's arm, made her way slowly to the Hobbses' rooms, she slanted a quick glance at him. The light overhead in the elevator alcove shone on his hair with the gleam of old gold coins and cast his features in bronze. It made him look remote, unfeeling, like an ancient idol seen from afar. The arm under her fingers had the hard support of a steel beam, and was just as impersonal. No, she must have been mistaken. Never by word or deed had Logan promised her anything, not ever.

Janine was slender and chic in a black jersey designer gown with draped lines and practically nonexistent shoulder straps. It was not a good color choice for her. It failed to make the most of her tan complexion and threw into relief the twin spots of color that burned in her cheeks.

"Come in," she cried as she opened the door to them. "I was about to send out a search party. Logan, how handsome you look, and you are pretty too, Clare, in that darling little dress. I do love it on you."

"Thank you," Clare said, her gray eyes clear. "It is one of my favorites."

Janine gave a trill of laughter that had a forced sound. "Do sit down, and Marvin will fix you a drink, won't you darling?"

Marvin Hobbs stood beside a small wet bar in one corner of the room. "What will you have?" he asked by way of greeting. Logan told him, then led Clare toward an armchair drawn up near a cocktail table at one side of the room. When she was seated, he moved to the near end of the couch that flanked her chair.

"Are you still favoring that ankle?" Janine inquired with a touch of acerbity. "I would have thought exercise was good for it."

"All in good time," Logan answered, "It won't mend overnight."

"Few things will," Hobbs said, and handed a glass of chilled white wine to Clare and a mixed drink to Janine before returning to the bar for the glasses for Logan and himself.

"I can't stand to be an invalid myself," Janine declared in an offhand manner. "I am generally so healthy it drives me wild."

A small silence fell. The woman sent a sharp glance from one to the other of those present, then lifted her glass and took a large, almost defiant swallow of her drink. The ice tinkled against the sides as she lowered it again, stopping only as she reached quickly to set the glass on the cocktail table and clench her hands in her lap.

Hobbs cleared his throat. "Are the drinks all right?"

Clare nodded, taking a small sip of her wine to prove it.

"Perfect," Logan answered.

"Well, let's not all talk at once, please!" Janine said, crossing one knee over the other as she forced a laugh. "I would have thought, no more than we have seen of each other these last few days, that we would have a thousand things to discuss."

"That's right," Hobbs said. "We haven't seen you on the lifts or trails a single time the last three days, Logan. I thought you were a real buff, out from dawn to dark. Have you burned out on it, or is there some other attraction keeping you in the lodge?"

Logan smiled at the other man's attempt at humor. "I'll go again when Clare can come with me."

"That's real love for you," Hobbs said on a chuckle.

"Yes, isn't it?" Janine said, reaching for her glass once more. "Somehow, though, I had the idea you were spending your time working on your screenplay. I think it was Marvin who told me you were changing the characters or something."

"No," Logan said shortly. "That's been done."

"You are through with it, then?"

"Yes."

Janine turned to her husband. "In that case, I don't see what we are waiting for, Marvin. Why don't you tell Logan what you brought him here to tell him?"

A frown of annoyance crossed Marvin Hobbs's face, then was gone. "I may as well," he said pleasantly. Moving to a briefcase that lay on a nearby table, he removed a set of papers and brought them back to where they sat, placing them in front of Logan.

"What is this?" Logan asked, reaching to pick up the legal documents.

"Can't you guess?" Janine asked, leaning toward him, her eyes bright. "It's the contract for your screenplay. Marvin has finally quit dragging his feet and agreed to get behind the project."

Logan sent her a hooded look. "I thought you were the one against it."

"No, not really. Oh, I will admit I was annoyed with you for leaving California in the middle of the discussions concerning it, but I have always been on your side. Come on and sign it so we can open the champagne."

"No hurry," Hobbs put in. "Take your time and read it first."

"I intend to," Logan said with a tight grin for the producer. Taking up the contract, he glanced at Clare, his blue eyes dark with what seemed to be reluctant elation. Clare let her lips curve in a warm smile. For an instant a corner of his mouth tugged upward in response; then he settled back.

Clare sipped her wine. Marvin Hobbs consulted Janine as to the time their table was reserved for dinner and got a snapped reply. At last Logan turned the last page.

"Three and a half million, ten percent of the gross, casting discretion, editing provisions, script consultation – couldn't have come closer to what I wanted if I had dictated it myself. It's a fine offer, Marvin."

"For a fine piece of property. I expect to make a lot of money on it, especially with you starring – and right up front during the promotional campaign."

"That last is included too, is it?"

"I'm afraid so, but I'm sure you have an extra interest in making this picture a success."

"You make it hard to refuse," Logan said, his tone dry.

"You are not going to turn the contract down?" Janine demanded, her voice rising to a shrill pitch. "Not after all I've done?"

Logan barely glanced at her. "No," he answered, his face bleak. "I'm not."

The pens were brought out. Logan slashed his name at the bottom of all copies of the contract, and Clare, as a matter of legality, witnessed his signature. When the papers were put away, Hobbs brought out the champagne, popped the cork, and poured it bubbling into chilled glasses.

"A toast," Janine cried, lifting her glass with such an impetuous gesture that the wine splashed over the rim. "To dreams that come true."

"I would rather drink to hard work that pays off," her husband said, "but I suppose it's all in how you look at it."

His wife sent him a scathing look, then drained her glass. As the others drank, she set her glass down and walked quickly to a closet in one wall. From it she took a large leather handbag and drew out what appeared to be a folded section of newspaper. Replacing the handbag, she turned toward them.

"Marvin is not the only one with a surprise," she said, the words coming out jerky and hard. "I was in Aspen this morning and stopped off at the supermarket for cigarettes. Guess what I found at the checkout counter? This!"

Unfolding the paper, she threw it down on the table. It was not a newspaper but a half-sized gossip sheet printed on newsprint. On the front was a blown-up picture of Logan. Grainy and faintly blurred, as if taken from a distance, it showed him coming from a hotel with a woman at his side. Emblazoned across it was the lead title: SNOWBOUND WITH LOGAN LONGCROSS: TWO DAYS OF LOVE, A PERSONAL ACCOUNT BY THE WOMAN WHO LIVED THEM. Inset in one corner was a smaller picture of his house overlooking the gorge covered with snow. The woman beside Logan was Clare.

Clare stared at the picture with a feeling of sickness in the pit of her stomach. It could not be. It could not, but there she was with Logan's hand under her elbow, and her hair, blown by the wind, clinging to the rough material of his coat for a look of unbelievable intimacy. When had it been taken? The morning they transferred from the hotel in Aspen to the lodge? It must have been. But who had written the story? Who had dared to write it?

Slowly Logan turned to look at Clare. In his eyes there burned an anger so fierce that she felt her heart leap in her chest.

"No," she whispered. "No, Logan, I didn't."

"A personal account? Besides, who else knew?"

"I don't know, but I did not write it," Clare repeated, her eyes level, and yet with a hint of pleading in their gray depths.

"Oh, come, Clare," Janine chided. "You

should be proud. What is all this modesty? This tabloid is a national publication. Your story will be read all over the United States."

The grim lines of Logan's mouth tightened.

"Janine . . ." Hobbs said warningly.

"Well, I must say I never expected this reaction," the woman said, ignoring her husband. "Where is your sense of humor, Logan? Things like this are written about actors and actresses every day. People in public life are fair game. If Clare had not written it, someone else would, and I don't doubt they would have done a much more shocking job of it. Maybe you ought to read the piece before you go off the deep end."

To have Janine champion her cause, even in error, was so unexpected that Clare sent her a questioning look. The other woman's smile was so coldly triumphant that Clare drew in her breath in sudden understanding. Who had known that she had spent two days in isolation with Logan? Other than Logan and herself, only Beverly and John, and Marvin and Janine were aware of the episode. And Janine had an excellent reason for wanting to cause a rift between Logan and the woman she thought he was going to marry. It was revenge.

"Two days of love," Logan said, his voice like a whiplash. "I don't have to read

it to know what it's like."

He spoke to Janine, but Clare knew his words were for her, their sting a reminder that there had been no love between them, and precious little friendliness, during those days.

"Really, Logan, don't be so old-fashioned!"

"I think," Janine's husband said deliberately, "that it would be better if we left Logan and Clare to thrash this out alone."

"Don't be silly! There's nothing to thrash out. Clare just wanted to let everybody know that she had caught the elusive Logan Longcross. She is proud of the fact that he is in love with her, and what woman wouldn't be? She used her talents to spread the news, and now Logan wants to make a big thing out of it. The only question is whether he means to shrug it off and go on, or if it is important enough to come between him and the woman he loves. Until he decides, talking will do no good. We may as well go on with our dinner."

Clare could endure no more. She got to her feet. "You will have to excuse me," she said, forcing the words through the tightness in her throat. "I am not hungry." She nearly fell as she put her weight on her injured ankle; then she recovered and began to move toward the door. Her teeth were clamped tight with pain and her determination not to limp.

"Wait," Logan said, coming up off the couch.

Clare paid no attention. Grasping the doorknob, she pulled the panel open and started along the lower balcony. Once she was out of sight, she swayed and put her hand out to the wall for support.

Logan strode from the room she had just left, closing on her with swift, silent steps to catch her arm. "Let me help you."

"Thank you, no," Clare said, pulling away.

"You'll fall and break your neck."

"That should suit you fine."

"I might prefer," he said grimly, "to break it myself."

"Leave me alone," Clare told him through her teeth, evading his outstretched hand. As she stepped back, her heel hung in the hem of her dress, and she winced, grabbing for the balcony railing.

Instantly he was upon her, scooping her into his arms. They closed around her like steel bands, clamping her to the hard planes of his chest. Stiff with rage, Clare allowed herself to be carried to the elevator. Once inside, Logan set her on her feet while he pressed the button. Clare, her hands clenched at her sides, stood behind him in silence as they rode upward.

"Will you accept my help, or am I going to

have to carry you again?" Logan grated when their floor was reached. Glaring at him, Clare took the arm he offered.

At her room, Logan unlocked the door and pushed it open. Clare stepped inside, and swung around without a word to close it.

"No, you don't." Catching the panel with the palm of his hand, he followed her into the room. The door vibrated in its frame as he slammed it behind him.

"What do you want?" Clare demanded, much more aware than she wanted to be of the acceleration of her heartbeats.

"We have some unfinished business."

"Since you won't believe what I tell you, I have nothing more to say to you."

"That's too bad, because I have something to say to you. I want to know why you did it. Were you afraid I would go back on my word? Or did you think you would get two articles out of this jaunt of yours? The one I had promised you and this other piece of sensational garbage?"

"You are the most unreasonable man I have ever met!"

"Unreasonable? What did you think I was going to say? Good going, Clare? Or maybe you didn't expect me to say anything, because you didn't expect to be here. Your accident has been an inconvenience in more ways than one, hasn't it? No wonder you have been so quiet lately. You expected to be gone by now. You thought you would be far away by the time the piece came out."

"That isn't the way it was at all." As he moved toward her with leashed violence in his stride, Clare took an involuntary step backward, coming up against the bed.

"Bravo! You deserve an award, do you know that? An Oscar at the very least. You should be the one before the cameras, not me. I've never seen honesty better done, or innocence."

"Is that so?" If he refused to believe her, why should she waste breath defending herself?

"Yes, it is. You had me believing you. I was actually fool enough to be taken in by your story of losing your way and stumbling on my house, in spite of all the evidence that showed plainly what you were after."

The contempt in his voice was as much for himself as it was for her. Clare stood still, assailed by pain at the knowledge he had given her.

"You were smart, I'll give you that," he went on. "Such fine outrage at my suspicious mind, such a brave acceptance of danger and hardship, and what a show of being willing to pitch in and make the best of things. I had never met a woman who could smile when she was afraid or hurt. And then there was your friend, your nice, convenient friend, who seemed more afraid for you than awestruck at your chances of getting a story out of me. That was a master stroke — or do you just have her fooled, the way you did me?"

"Logan, I —"

"No, let me finish. I haven't told you the best part. I was so certain you were real, so impressed with your open personality, your quiet and gentle strength, that I made you the model for the women in my script." His voice dropped a note, and he moved closer to her, reaching out. She flinched slightly, but he only smoothed a strand of her hair back over her shoulder. His tone softer, he went on. "I took what you said of women and drew on what I thought you were to mold my women as lovely and loving, with bright honor and a sense of privacy that protected what they felt from the snickering curiosity of the world. Isn't that funny?"

"No, no —"

"It is to me. Turns out, I didn't make them like you at all, I only made them the way they would have to be to please me. I did the same with you. I saw something in you that was never there."

"If you are determined to think I could have written that article, then you never saw me at all," Clare said, her voice strained. Swinging around, she stood with her back to him and her head held high to prevent the tears in her eyes from running down her cheeks.

"I wish I never had," he said, a hollow sound in his voice.

"So do I," she whispered.

The only reply was the sound of the door closing behind him.

What could she have said to make him believe her? Nothing. The evidence against her was too damning. Janine had seen to that.

Janine. Clare might have accused her, though the time to have done that was the minute she suspected her. And yet, with the evidence against Clare lying in front of the two men, how could she expect them to believe anything except that she was trying to shift the blame?

No, Janine had chosen the perfect form of revenge. She had repaid Clare for daring to come between her and the man she wanted, for every impertinent word and smile, every embarrassment, every moment of listening to Clare dictating terms to her. If she could not have Logan, then neither would Clare; that had been her promise, and she had made good on it. For all her tongue-in-cheek championing of Clare's right to publish the story of her sojourn with Logan, Janine had known he would be disgusted by the idea.

Clare had also made it possible for Janine to pursue Logan. While the contract was in jeopardy, he had tolerated her pretense of an affair. Now that it was signed, now that he had some idea of the lengths Janine would go to command his attention, he need do so no longer. Though Clare could not be sure, she suspected it was only Logan's compassion for Janine's need to pretend that had made him go along with her. Other men had used her, and though she had encouraged Logan to do the same, Logan was not like other men.

He had so much understanding, did Logan Longcross, and yet he still thought she had written such a piece of trash. How could he? Why couldn't he trust her? Why did he have to tear her down to Janine's level? She hated for it to end this way, with her guilt forever established in his mind. He would always think of her as the woman who had wormed her way into his life and profited from it.

There could be no doubt that this was the end. The screenplay was done, the contract signed, Logan was free of Janine. There was no need for her to stay, and in all truth she would just as soon not see Logan again. To have to face him over a breakfast table and make polite conversation as if nothing had happened was more than she could stand. There was no need for him to release her from this masquerade. She was under no obligation to remain. She would release herself. All it would take was a phone call. With a little care, he would not even know she had gone until morning.

12

Clare pushed her gloved hands deep into her coat pockets and ducked under the limb of a snow-laden spruce. The piled flakes sifted down, catching in her hair, but she did not mind. They were so light and dry, and soon she would be where there were none. Her ankle was nearly healed; this long walk in the woods proved it. She no longer had any excuse to linger. She was perfectly capable of making the long drive home, as soon as her car was ready. It was taking an unconscionably long time for the garage to get it fixed. She had called the day she had left the lodge and been told it would only be twenty-four hours before it was finished. That had been almost four days ago. It was beginning to look like she was going to have to call them again. There was a limit to how long she could trespass on Bev's hospitality.

Not that Bev minded; far from it. She had been great. She had appeared within the hour after Clare had called her from the lodge, before Logan had returned to his room. It had not been the easiest thing in the world, helping a semi-invalid leave a busy place like the lodge virtually unnoticed, but Bev had done it. At least they had managed to go without running into any of the people Clare most wanted to avoid: Marvin and Janine Hobbs, and most of all, Logan.

It had been impossible to keep what had happened from Bev. It had been nearly as difficult, once her friend knew, to keep her from racing back to the lodge and giving all concerned a piece of her mind. In a fine rage, she had railed at the perfidy of women of a certain type and the incredible shortsightedness of men, excepting her John, of course. She did not have to be told Clare was in love with Logan. That had been evident to her for days, she said. The only wonder was that Logan himself wasn't aware of it. He could not have the normal preoccupation with himself and his effect on others of most actors, or he would have guessed it long ago. It was odd, really, for if it wasn't his ego that was smarting at Clare's betrayal, why was he so upset? So his privacy had been violated? It was not the first time. As for his disillusion, it would not have made him so angry if it had not also hurt him — now, would it?

Clare only shook her head at such arguments. Bev had not been there when Logan had told her what he thought of her. She had not felt the fine cutting edge of his contempt.

Talking with Bev had helped Clare to decide what she was going to do once she was back home. Finally, after so many days, so many delays, she and her friend had been able to discuss Clare's articles. She had liked them, finding little to criticize, though Clare, at this point, was uncertain whether Bev sincerely thought they were that good or if she was being complimentary in order to distract Clare's thoughts. Much discussion was given over to Clare's choice of jobs, the real-estate office and free-lance writing, or a change to the women's section of one of the big dailies. In the end, Clare, prodded by the memory of the effects Logan had been able to achieve with his themes and characters, had decided to stay with office work for a while longer, writing in her spare time. People were more interesting than charity bazaars and weddings, even if being too close to them did bring pain. It was always possible that her skill with words could be turned in a new direction, toward the creation of fictional people, or else toward biography, in-depth studies of individuals and what made them act as they did. She was anxious to try, at any rate.

In truth, she was anxious to be gone. The sooner she returned to her old routine, to flat land and rain instead of mountains and snow, the better it would be. She could not begin to forget as long as she remained here. Everywhere she looked was something to evoke a memory: evergreens, slopes of snow, frozen streams, blue winter skies, snapping cold, or the warmth of blazing log fires — everything. Though she was annoyed with herself for it, Bev and John were most disturbing of all to Clare. Their affection toward each other, their good-humored teasing and casual intimacy, were sometimes more than she could bear.

Bev, almost as if she guessed what was troubling Clare, said nothing against her leaving. She did insist that Clare plan to come again in the summer, or else promise to try a skiing vacation again the next winter season. Clare did not commit herself. In six months or a year she might be able to face the prospect of a return; then again, she might not. The decision would have to wait until then.

Clare had walked quite a distance. Bev's cabin was not so isolated as Logan's chalet, but the road it was on ran past several houses, then curved away over a mountain meadow edged with forest land. Clare had followed the road, then crossed the snow-covered meadow to enter the woods. There was no chance of getting lost, not on such a clear day with her own tracks in the snow to guide her back to the road. Somewhere just ahead was an overlook that Bev had recommended as a destination, a high point that commanded a scenic view of the mountain range that included the peaks of Aspen, Buttermilk, and Snowmass. She hoped she came upon it soon. Already her ankle was beginning to feel the strain of climbing, and despite nearly two weeks at this high altitude, she still felt the urge for more oxygen in her lungs after exertion.

Topping a small rise, she came upon the railed overlook without warning. Her gaze swept out and over a deep canyon with snow-whitened, precipitous sides, and beyond it the saw-toothed peaks glistening icily in the sun with a background of far blue ranges. It was not quite the same view as from Logan's house, but it was so near that Clare felt the breath stop in her throat, and she was assailed by such pain she could not move.

Logan. She had tried to tell herself in these last few days that it was infatuation she felt for him. But surely nothing less than love could hurt like this? If it could, then she was ready to forgive Janine Hobbs for lashing out at whoever came between her and the man she wanted. For Clare, the only thing that made it supportable was the knowledge that, unlike Janine, she had never allowed Logan to guess how she felt. She could not have stood to have her emotions exposed to his ridicule, or worse, to his indifference.

Regardless, she was glad she had been given the chance to know Logan and to love him. Even if she had known it would turn out the way it had, she did not think she would have changed anything.

"Clare?"

The sound of her name, a single word in a certain voice, released her. She swung around, her gray eyes wide and filled with dread.

"Logan," she whispered.

He stepped from among the snowy evergreens and leafless gray aspens. He wore his down-filled navy nylon jacket. His blond hair, bare of covering, was ruffled by the light wind. The muscle in his jaw was ridged, and he hunched into his coat. His brilliant blue eyes held determination coupled with an uncharacteristic look of doubt.

"How are you, Clare?" he asked.

Clare disregarded the polite greeting. "How did you find me?"

"Beverly gave me the directions — after I convinced her I had no sinister intentions toward you. When you left the road at the meadows, I followed your trail."

Clare's lips tightened. "I have no idea how you got around Bev, but that doesn't matter. What I want to know is why."

"I didn't get around your friend, as you put it. I explained the reason I wanted to see you, and she thought you just might be interested in hearing it."

"All right, then," she said, looking away with a lift of her chin. "What is it?"

He did not reply immediately. Clare, her attention drawn by his silence, glanced back at him. He was staring at her, his eyes narrowed in a frown. As he met her inquiring gaze, he said abruptly, "Your car is ready. The garage called this morning."

"They called you?"

"I'm the one who notified them of where it was in the first place, if you will remember. I left my number at the hotel with them, and the call was transferred to the lodge."

"I see." She had given Beverly's number when she had called to ask about it earlier, but it must not have been placed with the original repair order. "You could have left the information with Bev. There was no need to come after me."

He ignored the last. "Until the garage called, I thought you had probably left the state."

"No."

"I was glad to hear it. There is still the small matter of an interview I promised to you that was never given."

"That . . . that's all right," Clare said, her control over her voice admirable.

"No, it isn't. The interview was in payment for several days of playing the role of my fiancée. You were good at the job. I owe you something, and I like to pay my debts."

"You don't owe me a thing."

"Because of the tabloid article?" he asked, a strange note in his voice.

"If you like." Clare gave a small shrug.

"I don't like," he answered, his voice rough, "because I know you never wrote that article."

Clare stared at him, searching his face in a suspension of belief, not quite daring to accept his words. The muscle tightened in his cheek once more; then abruptly he stepped toward her, pulling her against him, closing his arms around her.

"Oh, Clare, don't look at me like that," he said against her hair. "I am so sorry for the

266

things I said to you." His lips brushed her cheek; then he kissed her eyelids, which tasted slightly of the salt of her tears.

"But how do you know?" Clare asked in an attempt to slow her whirling senses.

Logan let his hold loosen so he could watch her expression. "I couldn't stop thinking of how you looked when you saw that paper, and of what you said. I found I wanted to believe you didn't write that article. After I read it, I was almost certain you could not have. I read some of your work, and the style of this piece was . . . totally different. But if you didn't write it, who did? I decided to find out. I made a few calls to people I know, but I was told the story had been called in to the paper by a woman who identified herself as Clare Thornton. I was told, however, that the woman had waived payment in return for an assurance that she would have a by-line. I know writers are proud, but that didn't sound like a deal a hungry free-lance would make. Looking into it further, I turned up one other lead. The man who had taken the picture of the two of us was the same photographer who had snapped Janine with me on the coast. I paid that enterprising gentleman a visit, and what do you think I found? Janine had paid him to take that picture of the two of us at the nightclub. What is more, she had called him with a hot tip about me and a girl at Snowmass. And it was Janine who had arranged for the photograph to be bought by the gossip sheet to go with the article she had provided for them."

Clare allowed herself a sigh of relief.

"You don't seem surprised."

"No," Clare said. "I knew I didn't write the article, but the list of people who were aware we had been together during the blizzard wasn't that long. Janine was the logical one to suspect. But wait, are you saying you have been to California and back since I saw you last?"

"That I have, and the odd thing is, I wasn't the only one. On the return flight from Los Angeles I had company. It was Marvin Hobbs. His errand had been the same as mine."

"Trying to find out who had written the article?"

"Exactly. While I was trying to be certain who was not responsible for it, he was making certain he knew who was. We had an interesting conversation while we were winging our way over the Rockies."

"Oh?" There was something in his tone that made Clare acutely uncomfortable.

"He confided to me that he was about to take Janine on a nice long cruise to the Bahamas, and while they were gone they were going to straighten out their marriage, one way or another, though he had hopes that away from the country, and away from outside influence, they could salvage something of their relationship. I wished him luck — though for which solution to his problem with Janine, I carefully didn't say."

"I can imagine," Clare said dryly.

"His problems were not the only subject of discussion. Marvin had some pointed observations to make concerning a conversation he had with you. It seems he somehow got the idea you had a special reason for being interested in my script, and in how I might have felt toward Janine."

"He didn't —"

"Yes, I am afraid he did. He told me you had admitted to him that you were in love with me."

Clare was still. There was nothing she could say, though the lashes shielding her eyes trembled slightly.

"I don't think Marvin would have mentioned it," Logan went on in a reflective tone, "if I hadn't said something which brought it to his mind. He appeared to think I had a right to know about it when I told him I meant to clear you of blame because I loved you."

"You what?" Her lashes swept up to reveal her startled gaze.

"Don't tell me you never guessed, my darling Clare, not after the lengths I went to, the things I put up with, to keep you with me. You didn't really think I needed to be protected from Janine, did you? Oh, I will admit the engagement was convenient, but it was never really necessary. It came about in the first place because I didn't like the way Marvin looked at you when he thought you had been my playmate while I was in hiding; it just went against the grain. Everything else followed when I discovered how much I would hate to part company with you. With Marvin and Janine and the business concerning the screenplay occupying my time, I knew there would be little left for my personal life. As your future husband, even in pretense, I could arrange to have you near me. I still wasn't sure that you hadn't dropped in on me for your own ends, but I was willing to overlook that, even to use it, so long as it allowed me to come to know you better."

"The thought occurred to me once or twice that you were extraordinarily patient with Janine for someone who was supposed to dislike her."

"Jealous, were you? No, why wouldn't I be

patient with her? If she stopped hounding me, you might have decided I didn't need you around any longer and gone on your way — with your promised interview."

"A bribe," she said, smoothing one finger over the nylon of his coat.

"It worked."

"Did it? I would have stayed without it though it was nice to have you supply me with a reason for being with you."

"That bit of honesty deserves some recognition," he said softly, and pressed a kiss of gentle passion to her parted lips.

When he raised his head, Clare, a shadow in her eyes, said in an unsteady voice, "Janine knew how I felt — I suppose because she felt the same. That is why she went to so much trouble to be rid of me."

"That is the one thing I have regretted most about involving you in this," he said, the pressure of his arms increasing. "If I had not kept you with me, you would never have been hurt. I died a thousand times before I could get back to you that day on the ski slope."

Clare drew a deep breath. "I made use of what Janine did to me, though. I think I should tell you that in spite of everything I have tried to do to convince you of my innocence, I have a scheming nature."

"Hobbs told me about your try at blackmail. He thought Janine was being suspiciously nice to him, and when he tackled her about it after the newspaper incident, the truth came out. He didn't blame you. He seemed to think you were driven to it for the sake of something you believed in, the screenplay and — just possibly — the man who wrote it. For some reason I am inclined to take the same lenient view."

"Even if it means I am not quite the material pioneer women were made of?"

"Does that still rankle?"

"Not really, since I might never have known you had ever thought so highly of me if it hadn't come out when you were angry."

"I would have told you sometime. I will tell you now that it is truer this minute than it ever was. You not only have the qualities I mentioned before, you have shown that you are willing to fight for what you believe in. That is something any pioneer woman worth her salt would certainly have needed. There is only one other virtue I wish you had."

Clare tilted her head, a steady inquiry in her gray eyes. "What is that?"

"The generosity to go on loving, despite the hurt I have given you."

"Oh, Logan," she said, a catch in her voice as

she met his eyes, seeing in their dark blue depths the reflection of his remorse and the promise of a recompense of love. "I do love you."

He caught her close once more, the breath swelling in his chest. "Don't ever leave me again," he said. "Stay with me always, as my wife."

Clare closed her eyes, letting her head rest on his shoulder. "The publicity will be terrible," she murmured, a trace of real horror in her voice.

"I can stand it, if you can."

"I suppose I will have to."

His arms tightened and he smoothed the soft silk of her hair that spilled down her back. "Of course, if you would prefer to write your own, I still might be persuaded to grant that interview."

Clare drew back to look at him. "Would you really let me do that?"

"If it is what you want."

There was a radiant smile in her eyes as she lifted her hands to clasp them behind his neck. "I think," she said slowly, "that there are other benefits to being your wife that I would enjoy more. All in all, I would rather live our life together than write about it."

The look in his eyes was warm with love. His

reply, though unspoken, was more than satisfactory. As they stood close together under the trees, the winter sun dropped lower, tinting the clouds in the west with rose and shedding a soft pink light over the blue-shadowed snow. They did not see it.